THE HATHAWAYS BOOK 1

KATHI S. BARTON

This is a work of fiction. Names, characters, places, and incidents are products of the author's imagination or are used fictitiously and are not to be construed as real. Any resemblance to actual events, locations, organizations, or persons, living or dead, is entirely coincidental.

World Castle Publishing, LLC
Pensacola, Florida
Copyright © 2024 Kathi S. Barton
Hardback ISBN: 9798301325410
Paperback ISBN: 9798891263208
eBook ISBN: 9798891263215
First Edition World Castle Publishing, LLC, December 9, 2024
http://www.worldcastlepublishing.com
Licensing Notes
Cover: Cover Designs by Karen
Cover-designs-by-karen.com
Editor: Karen Fuller

Chapter 1

Kahana spelled his name four times before he asked her for pen and paper so that he could write it down for her. If he didn't love his mother so much he might not have forgiven her for his name. He and his brothers believed her when she said that she'd picked their names from a baby book by picking a page number and then a number down in the names. At least he didn't end up with Penrod. His brother was never able to live that one down.

"Doctor Tattler is with a patient, Doctor Hathaway. If you'd like to have a seat, I'll let him know that you're here." He thanked her and went to find a seat in the over crowded office lobby. He hated doctors with a passion. Of course, he was one, so he thought that he had a better handle on them than most.

Thinking to himself, he was glad now that he'd not asked one of his brothers to go with him. He didn't know what they'd say right now if they knew that he was in the office of their family doctor waiting on the results of a biopsy that he'd had done several days ago. They'd more than likely pound his head in.

He might not have worried about it at all if not for helping an elderly woman with her end-of-life paperwork all because she'd left a mole on her shoulder go. Just like he'd done for the last few months when it appeared.

That afternoon, he'd scheduled himself a time to have it biopsied. The surgeon, David Kincade, said that he'd do it for him, and no one would be the wiser. Then, he was called out of town to do a special surgery for someone, and he asked him where he could send the results. The only other doctor that he trusted was their family physician, Elon Tattler.

After being weighed and his blood pressure taken, he was taken to a room. This office, like a great many of the offices, this one and his own, were connected to the hospital. All he'd had to do was go to work and leave his area before ending up in the one with Tattler. No need for him to drive anywhere as he was sure he'd have an accident as nervous as he was.

"Your pressure is up. I'm going to just think that it's some dame you've been eyeing rather than these results. Didn't I tell you it was nothing to worry about?" He said he'd feel a good deal better if he could have the professionals tell him. "You were never trusting as a child, Kahana. All right. Let's see what we got.

Instead of reading it to him, Tattler handed the envelope over to him. Pulling out the mostly blank sheets of paper, the words across the top said there was no sign of cancer. Lying his head back on the chair, he had to take several deep breaths before he thought he'd not shed the tears that were filling his eyes.

"You all right there, Kahana?" He nodded, and the tears broke free. "Had I known you were this nervous young man, I would have brought them to you last evening. I'm sorry about this. The report also states that your bloodwork came back clear of it as well. You'll need to keep that wound clean and dry for a few more days, but other than that, I think you're about as healthy as a horse."

"I wanted to believe you. I did. But you know how it is when you get something stuck in your head. There is no shaking it lose." Tattler asked him if he needed to call his parents and brothers. "I didn't tell them anything. I didn't want them to worry. I was doing enough of that on my own."

He looked shocked, and he asked him if he thought that wasn't right. "Not to tell your family is treading on thin ice, Kahana. They'll worry about you twice as much now because they'll believe that you're not as forthcoming as they had hoped. Trust me on this. They're going to find out. Someone is going to let it slip, and you're going to be in the doghouse for a long time."

"I never thought of that. My only concern is that my dad, you know about his recent illness. Mom's been fretting over him for the past couple of months. That's why I did it here and not someplace more specialized on this sort of biopsy." He told him that was good thinking, but he should have told at least his parents. "You're right. I'll tell them…we're all getting together tonight for dinner, so I'll tell them all then. I don't know what I was thinking now that you've pointed out to me how hard they'd take this."

"And if the results would have come back differently, they would have been doubly hurt knowing that you didn't tell them so they could get you treatments sooner. Or whatever goes on in the mind of parents." Tattler laughed. "My wife and I had no children, and I'm so old now that I don't remember even what it was like to be a child. Time sure does slip by, young man. Remember that. They're not going to be around forever, so enjoy them for as much time as you have."

He'd had his calendar cleared for the day so that he could deal with whatever was going to be told to him. Deciding that he was going to go and see his parents, he closed up the office, telling the nurses who worked for him that they could have the day off with pay. He made his way home. Lucky for him, he supposed, his parents rarely left the house through the weekend, and he'd have them all to himself. Kahana started perfecting the speech he was going to tell them. By the time he was at their home, he'd cried twice more and had an upset head. Not a headache but his head was stuffy and paining him because of what he was going to have to do.

He saw his dad first. Dad loved to work crosswords and was good at it. When he asked if mom was home, she came into the room and kissed him on the cheek when he hugged her. He didn't know how to start so he just started at the beginning.

I found this mole, or that's what I hoped it would be on my shoulder a couple of weeks ago." His mom started to cry, but she didn't say anything. "I had surgery just in the office of a friend of mine, and he sent it off to be tested. It's not cancer. Just a mole like I had hoped it would be."

"You didn't tell us because you were worried about me, weren't you." Though it was a statement, he told his parents that it was part of it. "I'm not sure if I want to know the rest. While I appreciate your reasons for not telling us when you found it, I'm still not happy that you didn't ask for our support when you did. We would have been there for you, son."

"I know that. I honestly did. I just wanted to…honestly, I just wanted to shelter you from bad news. I would have told you if it was cancer, I swear to you on that. Just that…well, I didn't want you to be fretting over me all the time." He'd meant it as a joke, but neither of them were laughing. "I was wrong in that. I know that now, Doc Tattler pointed out that I should have told you before."

"Would you have told us when you found

out that you didn't have cancer?" He told his mom that he'd thought not to worry them. "I see."

"Mom, please don't be upset with me. I just didn't want to worry you. And you would have too even though it came back noncancerous." He got up off of the chair he'd been sitting in and went to his mom. Bending down on his knees, he took both her hands into his. "I love you with all that I am. You know that, don't you? No other woman will ever be like you, and I'll more than likely never get married because I would be comparing them to you, and they'd surely fall short. I'm sorry I didn't tell you. I do wish now that I had."

"Because we're upset with you?" He said that wasn't it but that he didn't have anyone to lean on when he had not told anyone. "You didn't even tell your brothers? That's not like you. You share everything with them."

"I didn't because I didn't want them to worry either." He put his head on her lap and let the tears fall. "I've been an idiot in this. Please forgive me."

"You're not going to leave me soon. For that, I'm grateful." She yanked his head up from her lap and looked him in the eye. "You pull another stunt like this again, and I won't hesitate to take you out to the barn and beat your bottom. Do you understand me?"

"Yes, ma'am." She put her hands on his cheeks and then smacked him. "I deserve that and more."

"See that you remember that in the future. I'll not put up with your shenanigans again. Do you hear me?" He told her that he did, loud and clear. "Good. Now, as punishment, you're going to be peeling potatoes for dinner tonight. And we'll need a good many of them." She looked at him again. "I love you, Kahana. I hope you understand that in the future as well."

"As I said, no one will ever come between my love for you and dad. You're first in my book no matter what kind of person that I meet along the way to love or marry." She snorted at him and told him she couldn't wait until he met the right woman. "I don't care if I ever meet her, mom. I'm at my happiest just being your son."

He did have to peel potatoes. He didn't mind so much, but he was careful with the peeler he was using. The sucker was all kinds of sharp, and he didn't want to have to go get any kind of medical assistance after today. Besides, he was sure that his mom would knock him off the stool if he were to get hurt peeling some spuds.

Working in the kitchen with his mom was a rare treat. She didn't care for people in her domain when she was busy, but he had a feeling that she was all right with it today as he'd been hurt. That's what she'd think of it as too. That she'd not nearly lost him but that he'd been hurt and needed extra care today.

By the time he was finished making tea for tonight, his shoulder was hurting. Asking mom for something to take for it, had her sitting him down to see what had been done. As soon as she pulled the gauze back, her hiss of breath had him trying to turn to see it, too. From his angle, it looked all right to him.

"He cut you so deep. My goodness, I never… I'm assuming that the doctor knew what he was on about. He was, wasn't he?" He told her who had done it. "Well, I'm going to have to talk to him about this. It's not what I'd call pretty, is it?"

"It's swollen right now. I loved it, don't get me wrong, but doing all this extra stuff here is making it sore as well." She gave him two naproxen sodium and told him to drink plenty of liquids. He was fine with that, but then she sent him to see his dad. Not that he minded, really, but Dad was asleep, napping was something that he often did of late—so he took the couch, lying down on it and took a nap himself. He rarely got to do something like this during the daylight hours.

~*~

Axel didn't know what to think when Kahana stopped talking. He was sure that he'd missed a great deal after he said he'd had surgery to remove the mole and to have it tested. Looking around the room, he realized then that he'd missed a lot more than a few things. Everyone was crying.

"But you're all right now." Kahana nodded to Audon and told him that he was perfectly fine. "So you didn't tell us…why?"

"I didn't want anyone to worry." Audon pointed out that they could have held his hand or something. "I've been told that I should have told all of you. And he was right. But at the time, Dad was just getting home from his stroke. Everyone was worried about him, and I didn't want to stress anyone out. And before you ask, no I wouldn't have told you at all after getting the results. I would have if it had been cancerous, but not the way the results came back to me."

"You were being a selfish prick then." Mom told him to watch his language. "I am. Trust me, Mom, I am. I'm mad, and I want him to understand that."

"He's fine now. And we're all grateful for that, correct?" She looked at each one of them, and he could tell that she meant for that to happen. But he knew, too, that after they left their parents' house, he was going to knock his brother around a bit so that he—" There will be no retaliation later either, Axel. From any of you. I mean it."

They all nodded then she told them that she needed to hear their words. After telling her that they were all right with not beating the crap out of Kahana later wasn't really want he wanted to do, but he loved his parents and wouldn't go against their words to him no matter what.

After dinner, they all sat in the living room with Dad to watch some television. It hadn't occurred to him how old his parents were until Dad had his stroke. It was a small one, they all had been told, but there was still some damage to his heart, and it had terrified each and every one of them.

"Do you work tomorrow?" Axel had to think, then told Kahana no, he was off the entire weekend, too. "My offices are closed due to some work that's being done there, so do you wanna hit up some auctions with me?"

"Are there very many, or do you have one in mind?" Kahana handed him the listing that wasn't too far from where they were now. "This is the old Heathers house, isn't it? I thought that they'd already settled up where all the things were going to go."

"They didn't have a will, so it had to be in probate for about the last six months or so. The wife passed away while that was going on, and then they had to do the same for her. Figuring out who got what wasn't an issue because they only had one son, and he's in a nursing home. The money from this is supposed to go for his care there. I don't believe they had any life insurance, either. Besides, I can't really lift all that much so I thought you and I could get some stuff and you help me get it to my home. What I did today sent me into so much pain that I was nearly sick with it."

"I'm sorry about that. I'm still mad at you, but I love you. I'm so glad that things turned out the way that they did. I don't know what I'd do if anything were to happen to any of you." He said that he felt the same way and took back the listing to point out a couple of things on it.

"There are all kinds of things listed for the household. Trunks, too, that haven't been opened in decades, I heard. Also, there is a lawn mower that I'd like to look at. When I called to talk to the auctioneer, I was told that it only had about twenty-two miles on it." He asked him what that meant. "I'm not being a smart ass about this, but I had to look it up as well. It means it's only been driven for that amount of time. It was used on the flat ground around the house. I didn't know what that meant either until I asked. I guess if you have someone mowing your lawn for you, you never really know that kind of stuff.

About six months ago, their mom had kicked all of them out of the house. She'd not been mean about it but just wanted them out on their own. He got himself a condo. The others, with the exception of Stamos, had gotten a condo as well. He told his brother that he wished he'd gone the house way instead of living with a bunch of people surrounding him.

"Living in the dorms at college taught me that I wasn't going to be a good neighbor. The noise all the time and people just walking by my room talking. It was distracting all the time. Then there were the times that they got out of hand with their partying and had to have the police called."

"You didn't nark on them, did you?" He said it had been tempting but no, he'd not been the one that had called the police. "I know, too, that even to live off campus was crazy loud. I guess you would have thought that I'd have learned something from that. But I'm house hunting now. Not too much luck, but that's what I've been doing in my spare time."

In the end, they invited their mother to go with them. She didn't want to leave Dad alone, but Dad told her that he needed some peace and the outdoors, too. So, the four of them decided to meet up at their parents' home and then head to the auction. He was excited about that. Getting to spend time with his little brother and parents could be just what he needed to get himself out of the funk he'd been in the last couple of weeks.

Three weeks ago he'd broken it off with a woman that he'd been seeing for a few years. He had just grown bored with her constant whining about how much he worked. She was a partier as well. Nothing that he'd ever been a part of was the night life. But she'd taken it harder than he could have imagined and decided to sue him for breach of promise or something along those lines. He'd won the court case, which didn't make her happy, and that was when he realized that he wasn't as in love with her as he'd thought. She was...well, she was convenient. Someone that he could have hanging on his arm when going out and a sex partner when he needed that, too. However, now he was in a bit of a depression because he thought that he'd wasted several years with that woman, and he didn't have shit to show for it.

Axel didn't much care for his job either. He was working for a larger firm in the Columbus area and didn't think that he'd go any further than he was right now. He was an attorney of some notoriety as getting the things done for the clients. But he figured out and should have known better that all the people that he represented were scum balls and shits of the earth that once they were no longer considered in whatever brought them to court, then they would run out and do the same thing again. Christ, he hated people nowadays.

The next morning, he was up with the sunshine. He took a note from Kahana's book and decided to not just find himself a house but his own business front. Last night, after getting home, not only did he scan the listing again, but he also put in his two weeks' notice. Axel had enough personal time and vacation left that if they were to tell him that he wasn't needed the last two weeks, he'd be fine until he found something else.

His college debt was paid off, thanks mostly to the job but that's about all he had to show for that as well. Sure, he was good at it, but he didn't care for having to pay his boss for allowing him to work for them. He wanted his own money from now on.

Going to his parents' home, Mom was feeding Kahana a big breakfast, and he was just in time to get some of his own. He didn't care for vendor food as a whole, and auction food was usually the worst. Not that everyone who catered to the auctions served terrible food. But he'd been sick a couple of times and was glad that he'd not have to suffer anything when he got home from it.

They were early as usual. It was his mom

who liked to get to places early. He supposed that they'd all gotten that from her. She would arrive at some place they needed to be about thirty minutes earlier than it called for.

His parents liked biding on the box lots. They were, like they would be at any auction, spread out over the yard. He saw a couple of things that he wanted and asked his parents to let him know when they were coming up. He and Kahana went to where the tractors, seven of them, were being shown how well they were running by a few farmers that he knew. One of them was Hamilton Fitzpatrick.

About a year or so ago, Hamilton had defaulted on his loan with his own farm equipment. There were a great many people around who had tried to help the elderly farmer, but he wasn't having it. In the end, Axel had to serve papers to him and then wait around while the bank reposed not just his home and land but all his fancy tractors as well. He didn't know what he did nowadays, but he knew just how to get the bigger tractors started up and keep them running. Perhaps he worked for the auction house that was out and about today.

"Mr. Hathaway." He nodded at the man

and his wife. "Have you thrown any more old people out of their homes of late?" Before he could answer, not even sure what he'd say to the man, the auctioneer stepped between the two of them with his back facing him and Kahana.

"I told you before I don't want any trouble, Mr. Fitzpatrick. I also told you that if you were nasty to anyone, you might as well get your gear and get on home. I'll not have you pissing people off when they were only doing their job. You should have listened to these good people when they tried to help you. Everyone in town knows that. This is your second warning about this, and I won't have it. Go home."

"Damned lawyers." Fitzpatrick stomped away, nearly dragging his poor wife with him. The man was going to cause more trouble if he didn't miss his bet, and he would have to keep an eye on him. He and Kahana moved out of the area, no more interested in the bigger tractors than he was in his job. They were approached by Mr. Lundon when they went into the house, surprised at how much was in there with all the stuff on the lawn.

"I need your help if you're interested." It was Kahana who asked him what it was pertaining to.

He was handed a flyer that he didn't look at before the man started talking. "I gotta sell the house at noon. If no more people than this show up, I'm going to be giving all my profits away and not meet the payments on the boy's care. I didn't ask you first and should have started with that. Are you interested in the house? Either of you?"

"I am." He didn't know where that had come from as he *wasn't* interested in the house. But he did think about it now. It was within walking distance from his parents' home, close to the downtown area as well as the mall was still only about five miles away. He also liked that there were acres that came with the house that he'd never thought of before. According to the flyer he'd been handed, it was just over two hundred.

"Most of the land has been rented out to other farmers. They rotate their planting seasons by family. One sows winter wheat the other corn or potatoes, whatever they need at the time. It's been working out for them well, except for this sale has them in a tizzy, as you can imagine. They're afraid that if someone buys the land, they'll turn it into strip malls or those rental places where you can store your junk. That's what the people here did.

Had them four of those big ones, and that's what is out on the lawn. Christ, it was a nightmare setting up for this thing. They were hoarders. Every little scrap of something? They would put it into a pile. We only had to do the lower levels as neither one of them could climb the stairs, so that's a big plus."

"I will have to talk to my attorney." Since he was one anyway, he'd just pull the files that he needed and go from there. "It's only just eight-forty-five now. I'll get back to you as soon as I have it figured out."

The first thing he did was call the bank. He was told that the house needed to be completely overhauled before it would be livable. The banker also told him what he'd be paid in rent for the other parcels should he purchase it.

"It'll be pretty close to what you'd have in a house payment, Axel. Also, there is a store front that goes with the house. It's just another house converted into a business, but you can rent it out or use it too." He asked if he could put offices in the building. "Yes. There is plenty of room and believe it or not, plenty of parking as the building comes with the lots on either side of it. "And it's in the sale today? I don't want to hope for the houses only to find out that I bought the farm house and nothing else came with it."

"No, I assure you, Axel. The house that you're there with, the two hundred acres as well as the building downtown are all included in the sale today. Nothing is being split up." He asked a couple more questions, finding out that the furnace was new and there wasn't any kind of air conditioning in the place. "If you have any questions before the auction, I'm going to be there at ten to answer any questions bidders might have. You'll get a good deal, Axel, even if you never live in the houses. The land alone is worth that much."

After getting and estimate on what the property and houses would be worth on the market today, he had a headache. But he was going to buy the house so long as he could get a good deal on it. Renovating the house on the lower floors was going to be costly. He'd need a good deal on the house if he wanted to live there.

At ten o'clock, Mr. Bean showed up. He had more paperwork with him than he'd told him about, as well as the mineral rights to the farm. There was also a land map that he was free to look at, as well as the paperwork on the furnace and new roof that had been put on about three years ago. It was metal and would last for a good long time. He went to talk with his parents, knowing that they'd have information on the place that no one else would have.

"The missus, Opal Heathers, she just couldn't keep up with the house and land after Richard passed on. To be honest with you, I'm not sure how much they did to the place when he'd been alive, either. Mostly, they went back and forth to the nursing home to see their boy. I think he's about fiftyish now." Neither of his parents thought that the boy was able to live on his own. Even with his parents, he would have been a handful. "He has down syndrome as well as autism, poor boy."

"I think one Christmas, the ladies' club was going to the nursing home to sing carols. However, the *noise* that we were making, his nurse's words because the young man couldn't speak was too much for him, and we had to avoid the hall that he was in." Mr. Bean said it was a right shame that he was born like that. "I know that the Heathers couldn't have loved him more. But when they were getting up there in years, taking care of him was a bit much. And if I remember right, he was a big man…I guess he is our age now. Late fifties to early sixties."

Axel wasn't sure if he should bid on the furniture that was with the house. He didn't own it yet and he didn't have anywhere to put things until he did get himself a house. Being determined not to let himself get to worked up about it, he decided that if he didn't get the house, he'd just put the things that he'd gotten in storage and go that route.

Chapter 2

The house was a work of art. While doing a walk thru on it, keeping track of the work that had to be done on it with her tablet. Her dad, he was the one in charge and Mac was only his foreman on jobs like this one. Today, he was letting her figure out the price that it would cost to renovate the entire down stairs and three of the bedrooms on the second floor into something livable. She just wanted to find the man who owned the house and ask him if he had taken a look around at the wood and tilework that had already been laid.

"I heard tell that Mr. Hathaway, the one that bought this, got a good deal on it. I wonder how much of a deal he got. It's a big flipping house, don't you think, Mac?" She told him she didn't know, but he should be looking at the house itself and not the deal that he had gotten. "Yes, you're right. It sure would be a waste of good craftsmanship to just pull it all up and change it out with chrome and glass."

Neither one of them thought very much of modern houses. They'd work on them, even give the people a good deal on it. But they'd rather live in a home like this one than not. She even lived at home because she couldn't find herself a house that even came close to this one in what she loved.

"I used to come by here when I was about your age, honey. Just to see the old place. I think that's what made me go into construction was this one. I thought that if I could live in a house like this, I'd be a tinkerer rather than tinkering at other people's homes." He stopped so suddenly that she ran into him from behind. "There's a fireplace there if I don't miss my bet. See how the wall has about an eight-inch difference. And I'm betting too that those windows there are full length, and somebody just boarded them up from the inside. I'm going to have me a look see. You wait here, and I'll be back."

Smiling, Mac put her hand on the wall and knew that Dad would have had it right in saying that it was only eight inch difference. As soon as she heard him whooping it up, she knew that he'd been right. Not only was there a chimney, but the windows were just what he said. While she was waiting for him to return, someone came into the room she was in and asked her what she was doing here.

"I'm with Booth Renos and Construction. We're here to give an estimate on the house to do the work." He said that he was sorry that he'd had several run-ins with people wanting to get a look at the house since buying it. "You just assumed that I'm a trespasser even though I have a badge on my shirt as well as the name of the company on my back. That's not very nice of you, now is it?" She should just keep her mouth shut but she just wasn't able to do that. Not since she was old enough to speak.

"Don't get your panties in a twist. You wouldn't believe the people that come by here hoping to find a dead body around or something. I had people in the kitchen just last night trying their best to get out of here with the big counter in the middle of the room." She told him that she'd not been there yet. "You're doing estimates, correct?"

"My father and I are, yes." He told her again that he was sorry, so all she did was nod at him. The guy was an arrogant ass, and she immediately disliked him. If they got the job, she'd have to work with him, but she knew she didn't have to like him. "My dad went out to check on the windows in this room. He was sure that they were floor-to-ceiling ones."

"They are. I'm hoping that you'll be able to salvage as much as you can with the woodwork that's in this beauty rather than having to tear it out." She told him about the fire place. "A fire place? On this wall, you mean? No one else mentioned that to me."

Her dad joined them as she was pulling out her pocket knife to see what they were going to find. With Mr. Hathaway's permission, she cut through the wallpaper that was only the top layer to four more sheets of the stuff to find drywall. After cutting a hole in that, she could see that it was a beautifully done tiled-up chimney with a large, at least it looked that way to her, a large fireplace that looked like it was built and decorated just for this house.

"I'm betting that under this ugly carpet is tile work in the hearth, too." He helped her pull the carpet back, and there it was. The most beautiful tiled work of art that she'd seen. Pulling it back further, she wasn't the least bit surprised to find that the floor was oak with a darker wood, more than likely mahogany design going around the entire room that made her salivate to see it all in its glory. "Christ, this is wonderful. I'm guessing you want it covered up with something less hard and cold, am I right?"

"You're a prickly little thing, aren't you? No, I don't want carpet in any of the rooms. My mom told me that I'd have to get large area rugs for the bedrooms so that you don't have to step on a cold floor in the winter, but I disagree. Get some slippers if you think you're going to cover something up simply to keep your feet warmer.

Mac felt a little less angry with the man when he said that. He also wanted to know if there was a way to figure out how all the carpet was to be taken off the stair case. She went to the hallway that had the stairs going up to the upper two levels and leaned down to pull some if it off. It, too, was wood and not only that, it had stair runners on each side that had been in the house since it had been built. She did a little gig around the room when Mr. Hathaway said he wanted the carpet there gone as well.

"You like old things, I take it. I have a dining room and ten chairs that I'm having cleaned up. I don't know that anyone took a good scrubbing to the thing since they had their last meal on it. Also, don't even get me started on the beds I got. I was terrified that I wouldn't get the house and would be stuck with six sets of bedroom furniture and nowhere to put it." She asked him who was doing the work. "A company called Dixon is supposed to come out tomorrow and have a look at the stuff that's out in the barn. He was supposed to be here today but bailed on me. He said he forgot about the appointment."

"You should call Jamie…what is his name, honey?" She told her dad the last name when he asked her. "That's right. Jamie Girlington. He'll do you up right and won't be charging you a good deal more than he gives you an estimate for when he's finished too. Jamie and his family have been cleaning and restoring old furniture since…well, I don't remember. It's been a few decades, and they don't cut corners either. They'll do it up right."

Dad handed Mr. Hathaway one of the cards that he carried around with him all the time. He had a lot of business cards from people in many different kinds of renovations and would only recommend them if they were good people. And Dad would know. Her family had been in construction since before her dad had been born.

Dad and Mr. Hathaway started for the barn when she picked up her tablet again to start on this room. It made it easier to know that it wasn't going to be carpeted and the floors to be redone. It would be hard work but so worth it all.

"Aren't you coming?" She told Mr. Hathaway that she had to get some work done here for the deadline of tomorrow morning. "Oh, you've got the job. I have had ten or more companies come out here, and not one of them showed me the fireplace or the floors. I'd be stupid not to hire your company after you going the extra mile to show me that sort of thing, don't you agree?"

"Thank you. You still want to know how much it's going to cost, though." He said that they could work that out later. Right now he wanted her opinion on the furniture and if it was worth the cost to get them cleaned up. "Dixons don't need to know that we were talking about them, do they? I mean, it's hard enough in this business without pissing off someone that you may have to work with somewhere down the road."

"I understand completely. And while we're looking out there, if you could call Girlington and ask them to come out, I'd appreciate it." She told him that her dad had the cell phone and he'd gladly make the call. "You don't carry a cell phone?"

"Usually, yes. But not when we're on a job. Dad carries around this burner phone to call home and such, or in this case, someone to come out to a job site, but we don't want to be distracted by senseless phone calls while working." She went to the barn with her dad and Axel, what he begged her to call him to look around. Even the flipping barn was a beautiful piece of art.

Jamie showed up about the time she'd gotten to the bedroom furniture. She wanted it all. And the master bedroom set was the most beautiful piece that she'd ever seen. Just to touch the huge bed when it was raw like this was more than she ever could image happening. But to see it before and after…that was going to be epic for her.

It was nearly supper time when they finished up with the house. Axel walked around with the two of them after Jamie quoted a price on the furniture and was going to do that for the man.

Dad would point out things that he could see with his experience of older homes and she made notes about it on the company tablet. Axel then invited them out to dinner.

"I'm sorry, Axel, but we're having dinner at the house already. My wife, Dani, will about have it on the table when we get there as it is." Dad looked at her and she couldn't read his face. "Why don't you come to the house tonight. I know for a fact that there will be plenty of food. My son was going to be there but he's been called out of town as of this afternoon."

"I'd love that. Thank you very much." After giving him the address, she and her dad got ready to leave the house. She was going to have to have a talk to her dad about inviting strangers to the house, but he'd just laugh at her and tell her that it was his home, too. "I'll see you there in about half an hour if that's all right."

"Sure it is. Just come on down, and we'll have a nice meal together while Mac here figures out what it's going to cost you to have your house redone. It might take her a while. She's got herself a program on the computer at home that does the estimates right. Right down to how many nails it's going to cost us to do the work. My Mackenzie, she's brilliant."

Embarrassed now, she walked to the car. She didn't like compliments nor did she take criticism all that well either. But she'd keep her mouth shut and do what her dad wanted until the man left. She still didn't care for Axel but she really wanted the job for this house.

Mom met them at the door. She looked slightly upset but didn't say anything to her. She hoped that she was going to tell Axel he was on his own tonight, but all she did was welcome him with open arms and bid him to go to the library to wait for dinner to be ready.

"It's been a day, I'll tell you." Her mom was obviously upset because her Irish accent was stronger. "I've had to fire Mrs. Curtain and her daughter, Trina. Caught them stealing, I did. They were stealing right from the cupboard like it was something of a grocers. Oh, I tell you that I'm so mad that I could put a hex on them." At the shocked look on Axel's face, Mom laughed. "I don't be really going to do that. I'm only saying that because it makes me want to use a few choice words to them.

~*~

Axel couldn't believe how much fun he'd had having dinner with the Booths. At first, he wanted to smack Mac around for being snippy to her father, but he soon learned that they did this all the time. One of them would take a swipe at the other until they ran out of things to say. Then, the other would start. Dani seemed to be in a better mood after dinner and he couldn't have been more delighted when she told him about Mac and her construction experience.

"There she was, all of seven years old, taking down the drywall in her room. Wanted a bigger closet than the one she had in there. Not that I blame her. It was barely fit for a person to stand in it much less the clothing as well. Her daddy went in there ready to bust her bottom when she turned to him and told him she was going to use her birthday money to buy the drywall and would he please show her how to hang it. The two of them have been in business since. And the closet? Well, it's a right nice one, too. She doubled the space, and it only took her a couple of weeks to learn a new trade, hanging drywall."

"They were just bits and pieces that she

could do then. But she got the hang of it right quick. Never been as proud of her as I was that day. And I get more and more out of her daily when we're working." Charlie, what he insisted he call the other gentleman, put his hand on the back of Dani's chair while finishing his part of the tail. "Worked every job, too, that you have to work with reconstruction. Mac here can plum out a bathroom or kitchen and do the rewiring as well. You do understand that your house is going to need rewiring, at least in the kitchen, correct?"

"A heavier load is what one of the others quoted me. But all he said was that it was going to have to happen and didn't tell me that he'd do it." Both Charlie and Mac said, *Daniel Jefferson.* It shocked him when they knew which person had told him that. "Would he have done it?"

"No, sir. He might well have left it open for you to have someone else come in and do it, but you'd have to put that in writing for him. Also, if he tells you that he's going to need fifty sheets of drywall, then he'd only going to work until the fifty is gone. Won't go out of his way to tell you he needs at least another sheet of the stuff." The more he spoke with this family, the better he was feeling about telling them that they had the job. "Someone else you might want to watch out for is old man Trimble. Don't rightly know if you have silver that needs to be cleaned up but he's not too trustworthy about that sort of thing. He'll find you cheaper pieces and then tell you that is what you gave him to work on. After that, he'll fence it off for a much better deal after it's cleaned up. Now, I don't usually go around bad-mouthing my fellow reno guys, but I'd hate to see you ripped off when you've been a stand-up feller about your house."

"I can't thank you enough." It was Mac who told him about the lawn services. "I do have a lot of grass that needs to be cut, that's for sure."

"Also, you're renting out the land that would lay fallow if you didn't. I'd check my receipts on that, too, if I were you. I'm not saying that the realtor or whoever you purchased that house from is steering you wrong, but I'm betting that you don't get paid in the low months when there is no planting can be done."

"You think that they're only paying me in the productive months?" She said that she didn't know for sure, but she'd bet that was why the Heathers were having so many money problems.

"I'm assuming because it's doubtful to me that you have anything to gain about this that you're dead on the money. Do you think that the agency is in on it?"

"As I said, I don't know for sure, but they were biting at the bit to have that house to sell. If no one paid enough during the auction, the real estate company in town was going to be able to sell it for a large profit." He told her that he'd gotten it at the auction. "I figured as much. I'd keep an eye on your profits, Mr...Axel."

That was a great deal to digest, so he pulled out his phone and began making notes on things. He'd have his brother look into the information that he'd been given, Penrod being a homicide detective, and see where that landed him. He did wonder if Mr. Lundon was aware of things going on too.

It was nearly ten when he made his way home. He'd had such and enjoyable time at the house, and the food was so delicious that he found himself wanting to see what they had for breakfast. After he was shown the closet that Mac had fixed, it surprised him that she still lived at home and in the same room as a child. But then, when Charlie was walking him to his car, still talking about the things in the house that he'd loved, he asked him about Mac.

"Her name is Mackenzie Caroline Booth but she can't stand to be called that. Left at the alter she was literally left there by the man that we all thought was a good feller. But then I walked her right up to him, having the biggest odd smile on his face. He then took the time before leaving her to tell her that he only wanted to marry her on account of her having money. But there wasn't any. Or so he thought. Left her there to deal with all the fallout the little pisser did." Charlie laughed. "Her mother and I renewed our vows that day, had us the grandest party you've ever seen and she moved back home with us because she was heartbroken. Wouldn't know if to see her, but I could hear her crying at night, and then..." He snapped his fingers. "She was over him. I think that him getting arrested was a big factor in that. Donald Richardson is his name. He was a con artist she found out and watched him close enough that when he tried to get an elderly woman to turn all her funds over to him after they got married, he'd leave her high and dry. Turned out that was what he'd been planning to do with my Mac but she had him sign a prenup for again as he assumed was lots of money."

"I don't mean to be crass or anything, but is there a lot of money? You've hinted at that twice now." He laughed, it was like a barking sound that had him thinking that the man had been laughing all his life. "You're a good man, Charlie."

"Yes, sir, you are too. Me and my wife, not counting the businesses, own a house in about every country that there is. Insurance money, too, as well as a nice retirement bundle that we've never touched but put into every week. Millions. Mac has quite a bit more with her grannie leaving her all her money and a house too. She never liked me, but she did like our kids. Our son, Charles, he works for the government in real estate for them and makes a good living off that as well. He's married with a son and one on the way. And they have an extremely comfortable life. Neither of them would have to work for what he had, but he likes to stay busy. So does Milly, his wife."

He put out his hand and was happy that the man took it. He really had enjoyed his time with them and was glad that they had shown up while he was there. Axel was sure that he had chosen the right people for his house.

The next morning, he was up bright and early. He's slept well, too, knowing that his days were numbered in the condo. To have his own yard was something that he'd never considered before, and he was happy that he was getting a very large one. Turning on his computer, he opened the email from Booth construction. The estimate was a little higher than he thought it would be, but he knew nothing about this particular line of work. However, when he opened up the work sheet, he was surprised to find that Mac's dad had been right. There was a listing for nails in each room and how many they'd need to get the job done. If he was honest with himself, he'd say that was a great many nails but he didn't have any idea if that was a lot or not. It wasn't his area of expertise.

After making himself breakfast, he headed out. His thought was to go and find something to do, to keep himself busy while he worked out his two-week notice. But he found himself back at his house. There was already a construction crew on site, and he thought that he could learn a few things from them as well.

"Mac, she'll have the estimate from your home in town by tonight. She told me to tell you that if you want carpets and other items that you didn't have in the house, to let her know. She's going to assume, until she hears from you, that it will be the same in the building.

"I did want to go by there and have a look. I'm thinking right now I'm going to need to have it rewired as well. If for no other reason than the internet will need to be upgraded." Charlie told him to call the cable company and they'd drop off the wiring needed for that and that Mac could have it ready for them to hook up. "She is a jack of all trades, isn't she? Didn't your son want to go into business with you two?"

"He had his heart set on procurement for the government. His grandma was in charge of that when she'd been alive and he thought it was something that he could do. Worked out better than he thought. He met his Milly there one day and they've been in love since. Charles is a mite older than Mac. She was what they called a late-in-life baby. Couldn't be more in love with her if she'd been born right after her brother. There are eleven years between them."

On his way home that night, he had driven by the house in town. It had a sold sign on it, and he hoped it was his. To know that it was being worked on, too, made him feel like he'd done the right thing in buying the Heathers estate.

After being shown around the house that they said he'd be living in soon, he went back to the building downtown. It wasn't a bad hike to get to it from the house, but it would serve him well when the winter weather decided to keep the roads closed around town. At least he'd be able to work when things were down.

He found a crew of about ten men in the house. For whatever reason he was disappointed that he couldn't be in the house just with Mac. Axel wasn't even sure that he liked her all that much. She was caustic and a little bit hard on someone. He found her working in the second-floor rooms. When she glanced at him, not saying a word, he asked her how things were going.

"The plumbing in this house is new, so you won't have to worry about that. Also, the entire place has been rewired another thing you won't have to worry about either. However, while there is internet service here, it looks like instead of wiring it up in the walls, someone thought it was a good idea to just run lines from room to room by stapling the wire directly to the floor. Morons." He asked if she could fix that. "The true way to fix it would be to run it through the walls, but that would cause a lot of mess. Tearing out walls, even if it might need it, is always messy. However, there is a solution that can work as well. Tearing out only half of the walls to hook it from room to room and floor to floor. That's the way that I'd go. If someone trips over a wire, you'll lose everything."

She told him too about the windows on the second floor. They were in terrible shape and should be replaced with something more energy-efficient.

"Even doors inside the house could use a bit of updating. You're not planning on living here, are you?" He told her that he'd not. "I'd not take out the kitchen. Remodel and rewire it so that you have sufficient power if you want to run a microwave and the coffee machine at the same time. But if you're just going to use this for a breakroom of sorts, I'd not do much more than throw some paint on the cabinets and leave them. It'll save you a bundle doing that."

"All right." There were two half baths as well as two bathrooms in the house. He asked her about them. "While the demo is going on, however, you want the internet going in, I'd go ahead and take care that they're updated as well. Leave one of the bathrooms with a tub, but I'd put in a stall for the other one. And the two half baths, being on the first floor, I'd redo those since you might have clients using them as well."

He'd not thought of someone using his bathrooms. He didn't like sharing toilet space and thought that he'd be using one of the bathrooms on the second floor if he needed to go. But he would do as she said about the bathrooms, even enlarging the one by the garage so that he could have a small washer and dryer put in should he want it.

"You're thinking long term then. If I were to sell it, it would be better if the house was family-oriented rather than not." She said she was forever working with the assumption that the house or whatever might be going to someone else. "I like that idea. And while I'm at it, I think that I'll take care of the kitchen but last. If that's something that you can work into the project."

"You'll have to pick out some cabinets if

you want new ones, which is what you should be doing. And the flooring. Hard wood would wear better than carpet or even tile. Tile would be cheaper, but I have a feeling that you'd rather go with what it needs and damn the money part of it. If that's your thinking, you should step out of the living room area and look at the screened in porch. I'd not change that at all, but to put in new screens and better windows for winter. It's a lovely room that you could use for some of your clients too that need a breath for something."

He loved the way that she seemed to think outside the box and told her so. When one of the workers called for her, she told him she'd be back in a few minutes. That was when his brother Gilman showed up. He was just showing him around when they saw what the workers were doing.

"Dad told me that you were going to hang out your own shingle. Is that true?" He said that it was that he was sick of working for a firm. "If you want to have a partner in this venture, I'd like to rent some space from you as well. I could easily set up here and not be in your way."

"Don't you need to have a studio or something? I mean, I know very little about art and glass blowing but it would seem to me you'd not need an office space." His little brother laughed. "Tell me what you need. I don't care if you want to have space here. Just…the contractor is here now, and we can have her design the rooms for you. If you want."

"Absolutely. I'll get with him." He told Gilman that it was a her, not a him, and he laughed all the harder. "I'll have to be careful with that. I was assuming something that wasn't right, and that could get me castrated."

Gilman walked around the upper floor with Mac. He found himself trailing along, and when his brother asked Mac out, he wanted to smack him upside the head. Again, he didn't understand that. He still didn't like her very much.

Chapter 3

Mac had a pounding headache. It was pressure like she'd never experienced before. She was prone to migraines. Usually, she could just lie down for a little while, about an hour, and it would ease up. But this one. Not today.

She and her crew were going to start ripping up carpet in the downtown house. The other place, the estate home, is what they were calling the larger home. It made it easier, she thought, if they were to think of them as two separate jobs. She knew that it did her, but it wasn't really working out that way. When ordering, her dad ordered for both projects at the same time. That would work all right, but she thought that they should have been billed as two separate places.

"Want me to cancel the order, honey?" She said that it was all right. The equipment and supplies were going to be delivered to the estate house and she'd just have to have a crew go out there and bring it here. "They'd charge you nearly what it cost in the savings to have them separate them out and deliver them to each place, I'm betting."

"That's what they said to me when I called about the order. It's no biggie, Dad, I promise. I'm just dealing with this pain in my head, and I don't want to be a bitch about anything." He told her that she was doing a fine job of not taking it out on him. "I'm trying."

As the crew was getting some of the items that they needed to work on today, she found herself a dark corner and lay on the floor. It wouldn't be ideal for her to be there, it was dangerous, as a matter of fact, sleeping on the job, but she needed relief, and it wasn't going to come with her not being able to get to her doctor's or at least rest like she was planning to do. After about twenty minutes, she was ready to give up when one of the Hathaway men showed up.

"I'm Kahana." She told him good for him. His grin might have been cute if she wasn't in so much pain. "Your dad told me that you suffer from migraines. I can help you with that. If you'd allow me to."

"I have a doctor, but he's out of town right now. Usually, I get a shot of something in my head, I can't think right now, and that will do me for a while." He asked her what kind of meds did she get. "Let me think for a moment. It starts with a d...I can't remember."

"Dihydroergotamine? Or it's usually called DHE." She told him that was it. "That's usually for severe migraines. Has he ever tried giving you Sumatriptan? It's a lesser dose, but it might do the trick without making you sick. I heard too that you have a terrible tummy reaction with the DHE."

"Please, I'll take just about anything right now." He didn't waste any time but joined her in the room she was in. After taking her blood pressure, which was up a little, he injected the Sumatriptan right into her head and waited with her when it started to take effect. "That feels so much better already. Not gone but tolerable."

"I'll give you a second dose here in a few minutes. Just try to relax and breathe." He asked her if it was possible for her to go home to rest. "It would be but I drove myself in here today. I don't feel well enough to drive myself home."

After the second dose, she felt like she could

fly a kite. Or be the kite. She knew too that she wasn't going to be able to go home at all with the way that she was feeling. Just to stand up off the floor made her slightly ill; however, her head didn't bother her so much now. When he administered the third dose to take the effect all the way off her head, she couldn't have moved if her life depended on it.

Waking up in a dark room, she didn't move for fear of waking up her pounding head again. The longer she laid there the better she was feeling. It wasn't until her mom said her name that she realized that she wasn't alone in her room.

"You feeling better, honey?" She said she thought so. "Well, you've been down for four days. I don't know what you were given, but you sure did need the rest that went with it."

"Four days? Great. That's going to put us behind now." Mom told her to hush that it had been taken care of. "I think I can sit up now. Not too quickly, but I can sit up."

With her mom's help, she was not only able to sit up but she could sit in a chair as well. Her head wasn't hurting her at all, either. It was almost as if she were a real person today.

"With the shots that Doctor Gimble gave me,

it would be four or five days before my headache would go away. I've never felt this good, Mom, in a very long time." Mom told her because Doc Gimble was nearly seventy years old and told her once why mess with success. "I remember that. You wanted something stronger for your anti-depression, and that was his answer. I had forgotten about that."

"I didn't. Every time I take my medication, I think about that. Had it not been for your dad telling me to find a real head doctor, I do believe that's what he called her, then there is no telling where I'd be right now. I know that I'd be hiding away from people again."

Her mom had suffered terribly from depression. It got to the point that she wouldn't leave the house and didn't shower unless someone made her. And eating, too, was out of the question for her mom. She was still seeing her doctor and it seemed to have been a perfect fit for her. She might have to look for a doctor herself. Maybe Kahana would be her doctor as he seemed to have his head out of the past and working to be a better doctor than most.

After having some lunch with her mom, she

headed to the downtown building. A lot of work had been done while she'd been gone, and she was glad that the carpets were all torn out and the floors were being sanded. The work on the drywall was started but without the wire there, they were at a standstill for that.

"Did you call them to see what the holdup was?" Mark, her foreman just under her said that he'd called several times and was put on hold and forgotten. "I'll take care of them. I'm headed out that way here in a few minutes. I'll drop by. Is the company truck around?"

She was nearly there to bash in some heads when she heard from her dad. "They delivered too much here so when we get this finished up, then I'll send the rest to you. Damned contractors." She told him that she couldn't wait and was headed to the cable office anyway. "You tell them, honey. And I might just keep the cable that's going to be left over for their screwing things up."

There wasn't anyone in the office when she arrived at the cable company. After getting the run around for about twenty minutes, she finally had had enough and put her fingers into her mouth and let go of her infamous whistle. Dad told her that it could make trains look bad. It was so loud.

"I want the cable that was ordered a week ago delivered to this address." She carefully wrote out the instructions and what she needed. "If it's not here by the end of the day, then—"

"We delivered it three days ago." She asked the man who seemed to have a chip on his shoulder where he'd delivered it. "I'll have to look." When he didn't move, she took several steps in his direction, and that got him moving. "What will you do if we don't get it there by the end of the day? It's not like there is another cable company around to meet people's needs."

"Ah, but you're wrong on that. I'm thinking that from now on, I'm going to be telling people about satellite and the benefits that it will bring to their homes. Do you have any idea how many houses we work on that need an upgrade? What if we told them that it's better to go to a streaming service rather than depending on your company to get news and movies coming into their homes?" He told her to go ahead. "Good. I'll tell Mr. Hathaway that you're not going to be his provider, and that will make it so his brothers, all five of them, aren't going to use you either. Then there are the people that come to see them. How much business do you think you'll lose when they start telling people what a piece of work you are?" Mac made a decision she hoped that she'd not regret later. "You know what? Forget it. I'll just put a satellite in."

"Yeah? What are you going to tell that Hathaway person when it all goes to shit? You'll be begging me to come out to your little job site and put the cable in. You'll see." He walked away laughing, and she pulled out the phone and called Axel. After telling him everything that was going on, he told her that he was going to put her on hold, to hang on for a few minutes.

She could see the man she'd talked to answer his phone. Without a thought as to who he could be talking to, she made her way out of the offices and back to the parking lot. She hated being indoors more than she had to be, so she was glad for the small reprieve. It was then that Axel got back to her.

"Okay. If I don't miss my bet, Mr. Landry is going to be begging you to put the cable in. If he can't persuade you to do that, he's going to be out of a job. It's not your fault if that was where you were going with your thoughts. My dad owns the franchise here in town, so he's going to be making a couple of calls. If you think that satellite would be better, I'm all for it." She said she didn't want anyone to lose their job over this, but if anyone deserved it, it would be that prick. She also told him that cable internet was less spotty at times than having a dish atop your home. "Good, I was hoping you'd say that. I'm sure that within the hour, you'll have all the cable you need for several projects you have going on."

When Landry came out of the building, she could tell he was pissed. Telling Axel what he was doing, coming toward her had him laughing. Then out of nowhere, the punch to her face had her falling back on her ass, then nothing. She was sure that he was going to hurt her, too, when she was down. And she'd only just gotten her headache to go away.

Waking up, she wasn't surprised to see her parents in the emergency department room with her. What did surprise her was that Axel was there as well as Kahana. He was shining a light into her eyes, and it was annoying.

"Did you know that you talk to yourself when you're unconscious?" She told him that she didn't since she was out. "Good point. Anyway, I've had to have fourteen stitches put in the back of your head. Also, two in your lip. I believe, too, that you have a hard head. You should have had plenty more stitches than just the few that I was able to squeeze in."

"Gee, thanks." He laughed and told her that she was welcome. "When can I go home? I have a lot of crap that needs taking care of."

"You're not. At least tonight, you're not. As I was going to say, you have a concussion. As well as those stitches in your pretty head." She didn't think this day could get any worse than it was right now. "My dad has taken care of your cable guy. It's doubtful that he'll be able to work anywhere once this gets out. He's been arrested, too, by the way."

"Good. I've never met someone so arrogant in my life than that guy. How is it that he's been working there more than a day." Charlie said he'd never been told about him before. "Well, you need to make sure that whatever other businesses you own know that you're around to help them out if you need them. I'm betting, too, that the turnover rate for that place is high as well.

She was brought up to date about what was going on, and she was ready for them all to go away so that she could have something for the pain. As soon as she was thinking about how to be nice without feeling like shit, Kahana told her that she should take something for the pain. Thankful that it was taken out of her hands, she didn't have to be mean again and tell them all to get the fuck out. Her dad lingered a bit as she was drifting off.

"Baby, I just wanted to tell you how much I love you and am so proud of you." She smiled at her dad, the only thing that she was sure that he'd understand. "I'm going to leave when you're asleep. Don't scare me like this again." She nodded, then drifted off to a painless sleep.

~*~

"You like her." Axel looked at his brother, Stamos, and asked him what he was talking about. "I've never seen you like this before, and the only thing that has changed is that you met Mac. She is making you a lot less tense, too."

"I don't know what it is you're talking about." But he did. It just occurred to him that he loved hanging out with her no matter how prickly she was. He found that he wanted to say things to her that would get her going, and that was just stupid, he told himself. "She is the most odd woman I've ever met. She just tells it like she thinks too."

"Yes, she does. Are you going to ask her out? If not, then there is a long line of us that would love to take her out on a date." He felt his temper flare, and that surprised him. He'd not thought of Mac in that way before. "You're angry. Good. I was hoping that you'd get off your ass and see what the two of you can do together."

"I don't want to date her." Stamos called him a liar. "Okay, so I do but until you mentioned it, I never thought of her like that before."

"Now that you are thinking about her, I'm serious when I say if you wait too long, every one of us is going to ask her out. Doubtful that she'd go, she might not even go when you ask her, but I think that the two of you are more suited than any of the rest of us." He asked him what he meant. "I really don't know either, but I can see the two of you having a long-term relationship—perhaps even going the extra mile and marrying. Your kids would be hellions. But they'd be well loved and taken care of."

"I don't know what to say." Stamos told him to ask her out. "I think I will. She'll more than likely turn me down, but I'm not going to give up so easily. How did you get to be so smart?"

He knew that she was going to be at the downtown building today. She was supposed to be taking it easy, but he knew that he'd be doing the same thing. Working kept the demons away. Overthinking was his biggest problem, as was overworking. Taking a trip to the building, he was shocked to see how much had been done. Asking where Mac was, they told him that she was on the second floor pluming in the new shower stall that had finally arrived.

She was working when he found her. Cursing too. She was funny when she was flustered, but he didn't comment on that. He liked his head right where it was. As soon as she stepped back from the job, he cleared his throat. Almost as if she knew that he'd been there, she turned around and asked him if he really needed to have hot and cold water in the shower.

"I'm reasonably sure that I'd need them both. The thought of taking a shower with only one of those sounds very painful. Would you have dinner with me tonight?" She asked him what he said. "The shower? I'd really like to have both hot and cold if you can manage it."

"No, the other part. Where you asked me out. Are you insane?" Axel told her that there were days that he'd asked himself that same question. "I'm not much of a dating person. I mean, it's been a long time. I was hurt once, and the thought of getting tangled up with a man again has me a bit gun-shy."

"Your dad told me about Richardson. He seemed to think that you were also kind of glad that he left when he did." She nodded and cocked her head, and looked at him. "Do I have something in my teeth?"

"No. You really are an odd man. Where would we be going on this date if I were to say yes?" He asked her where she wanted to go. "I don't care, but I think I'd like to go to a place that has cloth napkins. I'm sick to death of fast food."

"I can arrange that. What time are you getting off today?" She told him that it wouldn't be too much longer after five. "Good. I'll pick you up at six, and we can have dinner together."

"You know, when your brother Kahana

asked me out, he said that I'd have to figure out where I'd like to go, and he'd take me. I don't want to have to pick everything out. If I were to ask you out, then I'd pick, but since you...never mind. You must think I'm off my noodle." He told her that he didn't think that at all that it made sense to him. "Thanks. I'll see you...I live with my parents, as you know, so don't expect to be able to spend the night or anything. And your home isn't up to par yet so no hanky-panky until we get to know one another a bit more."

"I can handle that too." He gave her a quick kiss on her mouth, careful of her stitched-up lip, and before she could chastise him for it, he left her to finish up her work. Now, all he had to do was sometime in the next six hours, he had to find someplace that had cloth napkins. He didn't think that would be so difficult. Pulling out his phone, he called his mom. She'd know the perfect place. He didn't know how she'd take him dating Mac, but it was only a date between them and nothing more. "Mom? It's Axel. I have a date tonight with Mac, and the only stipulation that I have from her is that there needs to be cloth napkins. I'm assuming that counts out all the fast food places around."

"I should hope so. Cloth napkins, huh? How about I think about that and call you back? Did she tell you if she's allergic to anything?" Axel told his mom that he'd not asked. "Might want to get with her mom then. Find out that and her favorite food."

"You don't seem surprised that I've asked her out." Mom told him that she was glad that he was getting out there and that she and his dad really enjoyed being around Mac. "It's nothing serious. I swear. Just that I'd like to see her, and this might not be anything at all."

"I understand that. But do you?" He asked her what she meant. "Axel, you've been hanging out with her since you met her. You've been to that job site more times than I think you've been to your own home being taken care of. Of course, you like her."

"Thanks, Mom. I'll call her mom right now. I just want this to be special. Don't ask me why, I don't have an answer but I do want to make this date better than she's had before." She told him that she'd be awaiting his call and to not screw this up. "I won't. I swear it. I really am excited about this, and I don't know why either."

After talking to Dani, she told him that when Mac wanted cloth napkins, that usually meant comfort food. Or steak. While she wasn't a big red meat eater, she did like a good steak on occasion and her favorite side dish was baked sweet potato. He thanked her a great deal, and again, she didn't seem to be surprised that he'd asked her out. Was he that obvious?

Calling his mom back, she had two names of restaurants that she thought would suit the bill. He told her too that her mother said that she didn't care for over-the-elegance when dating, not unless it was a celebration of some sort.

"That's what your dad told me when I mentioned that you were going out. That she'd be more of a woman that didn't care for that sort of stuff but would fine with paintings for sale on the walls sort of restaurant." Axel asked her if she thought him dating her was a bad idea since she was working for him. "Axel, you're a grown man. You should be able to figure that one out on your own. Do you like her, or are you just hoping to get into her panties?"

"I don't think that's the reason, no. I'm going to tell you the truth mom, the thought of her dating or even seeing someone else has me wanting to find them and tell them to back off. And I've never had a date with her yet. Is that insane?" She laughed, and he felt his own humor tugging at his mouth. "I'm going to take that as a no. You don't think that I'm insane."

"You'd be correct." She laughed a bit more. "I do see you two having a long-term thing. Will it result in marriage? I don't know. But I do want you to know that you have my blessings."

"Thanks, Mom. You're the best, and I love you very much." She told him that she loved him as well and that he needed to get his ass in gear before their date was on. "I was going to get her flowers, but I have a feeling, like me, she'd not want to see them die. Now that I think about it, I'm not going to get anything. It's our first date and I don't want her to be upset with me over a box of chocolates or even some kind of flower arrangement.

When he closed his phone, he thought about where they were going. He didn't think that it was a sexy dress kind of place, but he did want to see her in a dress. While sitting at the light in town, the only one, he thought about what she'd look like in something tight-fitting and red. When the car behind him blared on their horn, he realized that he had a hard-on. Things were getting out of hand.

Axel hadn't been a person that was a big dater. He did enjoy the company of the opposite sex and, on occasion did think about that when going out. But he found himself wanting more than that with Mac. He thought that she could hold her own in any kind of conversation and wouldn't speak if she had nothing to say. She wouldn't mince words either but tell him what she thought of him no matter what the circumstances were.

By the time six rolled around he had himself in a tizzy. He'd been out before, with beautiful women, too, but this date—he didn't want to put too much thought into what that meant, but he wanted things to progress to some other level with Mac. Not necessarily sex, but close to it. The thought of some heavy petting, like he was in high school, did appeal to him a great deal. He left to pick her up at a quarter past six and was glad that he'd not arrived too early.

She was still getting ready, he was told, when he was let into her family home. Charlie said that he was glad to see them both together but promised not to look into things too deeply. His smile said something differently and Axel laughed. Sitting in the living room with her parents, they told him how well his home was coming along. He was glad that someone knew, as he'd not been out there since he'd been the first day. Christ, he needed to get out more. Especially since he was paying so much to have the house finished up before fall.

He heard her in the hall before she entered the room. He closed his eyes for a moment, unsure in that moment why he'd asked her out. But as soon as he opened his eyes, it was all he could think about was how much he wanted the things between them to go the extra step. He wasn't entirely sure what that step would be, but he wanted to go there with Mac.

"You look beautiful." She told him to behave. "I am, I promise." She had on a dress, but it was far from what other women he'd dated had worn when out with him. Her dress wasn't short, but it was longer in the back. There were tiny strings holding it up with just enough lacy ruffle to hide the fact that she was wearing a bra. Having her shoes in her hand when she'd gotten to the living room, he laughed when he saw that they were tennis shoes. Axel was glad that he'd only worn jeans and a shirt and tie as he felt like they did well together on what they were wearing.

Getting into his car after helping her into the passenger side, he had to take several deep breaths before he got in as well. She asked him if he was all right as soon as he got the car started up. He looked at her and smiled.

"I'm not sure. I'm not even sure that I've ever been all right. But this, going out with you is going to be the highlight of my life." He kissed her again, this time letting himself linger just enough that she knew that it was more serious than the first time he kissed her. When Mac put her hand on his arm, he turned off the car and pulled her into his arms to deepen the kiss — still careful of her mouth. It was awkward, but it didn't seem that either of them cared. When they pulled apart, he was glad to see that she was breathing as hard as he was and had the same confusion on her face that he was feeling. "I don't know what's going to happen, but please don't date my brothers."

"I won't." He nodded and started the car again. They were pulling out of the drive when she spoke again. "I've been asked by them all, so you know. And it wasn't until you asked me that I realized that I was waiting on you to get your ass in gear and ask me out too. What took you so long?"

"I don't know. But I was stupid for not asking sooner." She laughed, and he did as well. "You know, you could have asked me out. That would have been fine with me, too. Then you could have picked where we go."

"Next time. Where are we going, anyway?" He told her. "That's one of my favorite places to go. Mom said that you called her and I'm really glad that you did. Thank you for wanting this to be special tonight. I'm looking forward to having a great time."

And just like that, he was in love. It took his befuddled mind to catch up with his heart, but there it was for him to see. He was in love with Mac.

Chapter 4

The date was going better than she could have hoped for. He was charming but not overly so. He was great at conversations and didn't push her to answer anything that she didn't want to, like talking about Richardson. He'd not brought him up; she had, and when she'd told him that the man was still in jail, he seemed disappointed about that. Mac had an idea that Richardson wouldn't have been long out before someone took him to task. But being in jail? It was a place that he deserved to be more than anyone else that she could think of.

The thing about the date that had her really liking Axel was when she got dessert, he didn't. Nor did he take any of hers. Not until she offered anyway. That showed that she could control what happened between them. Why that was even a thought, she didn't know but she didn't want to give up her control of situations when all around her was out of control.

"Your dad was telling me that two of the bedrooms upstairs are finished up. The wiring I guess you'd done." She told him how she had done it during the night. She didn't sleep all that much. "I don't either, as a matter of fact. I never have my mom told me once."

"I can work better in a room without having several thousand interruptions going on all the time. When there is a crew around, they'll make it their mission to find me and ask me all the questions they had in an hour that they'd been saving up all week or something." He asked about the cable issue. "Thanks to your dad, several people at the cable company have been fired. Which is good as he'd found out that—wouldn't he have told you this?"

"I, for the most part, stay out of the way of my parents' businesses. I'll help them out if they need a heavy but for the most part, they run the cable company as well as several other places on their own. It works out well for us all." She asked him if he had all that many businesses. "Yes. I have a partnership in the grocery store. Not that I have a lot to do with that other than to fix the occasional issue they might have. Several years ago, it burnt to the ground, and I did take out a loan to have it rebuilt. It's a nice little country store, and I love going there when I need groceries. Not that I have all that many needs for foodstuffs. I usually eat fast food or dine with my parents. I think that all of us eat with them several times a week."

When they were finished up, and the bill was brought to them, Mac wanted to snatch it from Axel and pay it for herself. She didn't want any entanglements that happened with a man paying the check. When they were leaving the table after it was paid, she was glad now that she'd allowed him to pay for her dinner. Axel told her that when he or she asked the other out, it was the person who also paid the bill. She liked that.

The evening was still warm out, so they decided to take a walk around the town. There really wasn't that much to see, but it felt good when Axel reached for her hand. She told herself not to get used to this sort of treatment and that it was only the first date. But almost as soon as she thought that, she let it go. He would be a romantic no matter how long they'd be married.

That thought had her stopping so abruptly that she nearly tripped over the chair that was directly in front of her. She looked at Axel when he said her name.

"Are you all right? You look like you've seen a ghost. Is everything all right?" She shook her head, meaning that she didn't want to talk about it, but he asked her again, coming to her to wrap his arms around her while holding her. "Tell me what's the matter and I'll try my best to fix it for you."

"I thought about us marrying." He paused for just a second before asking her if she was proposing to him. "And what if I am? Would you say to me?" Axel tucked her head under his chin and held her until he spoke.

"I'd say yes, of course. But you'd have to help with the house by picking out colors. I'm not going to have carpets put in, but there are about a million billion questions that need answers to that I'm not sure how to answer." She looked up at him to see if he was teasing her. "I'm not. Teasing you, I mean. I've been thinking about you a great deal for the past several days. And I've fallen in love with you too. You do love me, don't you?"

"I'm not sure. I mean, if what I'm feeling right now—it's nothing I've ever felt before, but if this is love, I can get on board with it." He didn't let her go but continued to hold her until people were coming out of one of the little diners that were sprinkled all over town. It didn't bother her that they'd been caught in an embrace, just the opposite. She felt like she could shout from the rooftops how lucky she was feeling. "What do you think about us heading back to wherever you live and having some sexy time?"

He picked her up in his arms and swung her around. They were both laughing when he sat her down on her feet, and she wanted so much to rush home and have all-night sex with Axel before he changed his mind about...about whatever they were feeling for each other. It was much too soon, she thought that they should be making marriage plans, but she found she didn't care. It was perfect for the two of them.

They walked around the area for another hour. It wasn't that there was anyone out that would talk to them but they did enjoy the privacy of it all, her especially. There were times when she thought that too many people were up in the business of people that they had no right to. She wanted her life to be hers and not plastered all over the place on social media, not that she had any accounts, but it was their business what they did, and she wished more people would realize that.

On the way back to the car, he said that he was going to take her straight home. She was sorely disappointed but didn't say anything. She had a feeling that he'd been thinking about what she'd said to him, and he was beginning to have second thoughts.

"I don't know what's going on in your head right now, but it's not terrible. Or as terrible as you seem to be making it out to be. I'm taking you home because I've only just realized that I only have a twin bed at the condo as my mattress is being cleaned." She asked him if he was serious. "I am. Had you asked me a month ago if it was possible, I would have said no. But now that I know, even my brothers are having their mattresses cleaned up. It's supposed to lengthen the life of the mattress and to help with allergens."

"I need a new mattress. I've been saying that for five years, but I just haven't done it. I'm worried that once I get it home, then it's going to be my bed for the next five years or so. Even if it's lumpy." He told her that he had the same problem, and that was why he had his cleaned. "I'll keep that in mind when I finally have time to look for one. I'd like to say that I do buy pillows but I don't do well with that either. Right now, I have about a half dozen pillows on my bed because whenever I buy one, it's not right. Even if I buy the same brand that I love sleeping on, it's not right."

"Next time I'm in town, we'll have to go to the store to look for one for us both. I'm in the same boat as you. The issue that I have is my cleaning lady. When she changes the sheets, she doesn't know which one I sleep on, and it'll take me to get her to return sometimes to find the one I love. I think that I'd be better off just having some random person picking out those things for me and tell me I have to live with it. It might save me a bundle."

They talked about anything and everything while they were driving back to her house. Once there, she couldn't believe how late it was and used her key to get in so as not to wake her parents. As soon as he kissed her goodnight, a long and drawn-out wonderful kiss, she slipped inside so they'd not be tempted to have sex on the front lawn.

Once she was inside, she leaned back against the door and smiled. It was perfect this night. And she couldn't wait until tomorrow to see if it was just a fluke or did they really love each other. Resolved to not bring it up first, she was nearly to the stairs when her dad said her name from the living room.

"You didn't have to wait up for me, Dad? I had my key." He said that he'd had to take a call and decided that he couldn't go to sleep right away. "Something wrong? I know that usually the service only puts through important calls when you guys go to bed."

"Your grandma Booth is coming to town. She should be here in a few days." All she could think about was if she had enough time to move out and into her own place. "I'm hoping that with you here, she'll keep herself out of my business and into yours. You have no trouble telling her to mind her own business."

"I don't. And I'd be glad to. Why is she coming here? I'm assuming that she wants to stay here when she arrives." He said that she was going to stay with them. She'd made that perfectly clear. "I can't believe that you're related to her dad. The two of you are so different. You must take after

Grandpa Booth more than her."

"I did, as a matter of fact. My dad used to tell me that it was easier to give in to her demands rather than fight with her. But he wished that he'd been less of a beaten man as he got older and realized what sort of person she was. Your mom seems to think that she nagged your grandpa to death, and that was why he died young. That's why I taught you to be as outspoken as you need to be around her." She told him that she didn't want her in her business either but wouldn't allow her to take over. "Good. If you'd not mind telling the Hathaway's that as well, I'd appreciate it. I don't want them changing themselves just because Hanna happens to be my mother. I don't much care for her myself."

"What time is she supposed to arrive? I was thinking that we should have Charles over with his family. I know how much she just loves children." They both laughed, and Dad told her that she was to arrive around five tomorrow evening. "Good. We'll have the Hathaways over and Charles and Milly and have a grand old time. Did she say why she was coming around now?"

"No, she didn't. But I have a feeling that it

has to do with money. The very fact that my dad put her on a budget makes me think she wants to up her allowance." She asked him if he would. "No. I will follow my dad's instructions no matter how much she bitches about it."

"Good for you, Dad. I won't allow her to talk to Mom the way she used to, either. Mom won't say anything, but as you pointed out, I don't have that issue." He kissed her on the cheek, and he stared at her for a moment too long for her comfort. "What? Do I have food on my face?"

"No, nothing like that, but you do smell of Axel. He wears that old cologne that I think my dad used. Old Spice, I think. Can I assume that the date went well? Will you be seeing more of him?" She nodded and couldn't help the smile that she could feel all over her face. "Good for the two of you. I'm so happy for you both. You both need each other. And I think that he'd make a good man for you to depend on as well."

"I wasn't sure if I wanted to tell you how I feel about him. I was afraid that you'd make fun of me or something. But I've fallen in love with him. I think. I've never felt this way before." He told her that love and being in love looked good on her.

"Thanks, Dad. But the real test will be tomorrow when he meets Grandmother. I just noticed that I have called her that all my life. Grandpa was Grandpa. But she was nothing more than Grandmother my whole life. That's very telling if you were to ask me."

She called Axel on her way up to her room. Warning him first that she was coming to town but also what sort of grandmother she was as well as asking him if he thought his entire family would come over for dinner tomorrow evening.

"I'll ask. I don't see any reason that my parents won't come, but I'll have to see if my brothers are busy. They haven't found anyone to love like I have." She giggled and felt embarrassed by it. "You're so lovely. I can't wait to see you again tomorrow. But if I'm going to make court at seven in the morning, I need to get my sleep. I love you, Mac. Very much."

"And I love you." When she put her phone on the charger, she laughed when she saw what came up. It was a cartoon bear blowing kisses at her. Getting into bed after changing, she figured that she was about as ready as she'd ever be for her grandmother, the old bitch.

~*~

It wasn't like he was meeting the family for the first time. The only person that Axel didn't know was Charles, but they immediately bonded when he was handed his little boy. Little Chuck, as he was called, didn't scream and yell at him like most kids did that he'd been around. He thought that it was because he was so big. But so was Charles. Plus, he could see some of Mac in his face, too. When he touched his hand to his cheek, he laughed like he'd found something funny about him.

"Have you met Dragon Lady?" He laughed, asking him if he meant his grandmother. "I do. She's forever picking fights with everyone so that she can be the poor victim. Milly can't stand her, and since we first met, she has kept her mouth shut when it comes to her. I tell her all the time to tell her off, but she is afraid that Mom and Dad will hold something against her. I think most of the time, they love her more than me."

"My grandma was wonderful. She passed away right after Stamos was born, and he didn't get to see her as we all did. But she would come by the house and pick out a couple of us to have an adventure with her. We never were jealous of the others that got to go. She made those kind of dates with us all the time. I learned how to order from her and also how to be a romantic. Believe it or not, she had me reading romance books when I was in second grade, and Mary, I don't remember her last name, punched me in the face when I laughed at her. I can't even remember — she caught a softball bare-handed. That's what it was. She was crying because it hurt so much."

"My grandma on my mom's side was wonderful, too. She lived on a farm that had all sorts of animals that city children never get to be around. I know how to milk a cow and feed the hogs, as she said it. Plus, I can drive a tractor." He laughed and said that it's not at all like driving a mower like people think. "She's been gone for a while now. And I find I'm sad that my children won't get to be around her and the farm."

"That's something that I've never thought about." He glanced over at Mac before looking at her brother. "I'm in love with your sister. I want you to know that."

"It's as apparent as the nose on your face. So if you're thinking of keeping it a secret, the cat is out of the bag." Again, they both laughed, and that was when the front doorbell rang. Ms. Booth wasn't going to arrive for another hour or so, but Mac told him not to be too surprised if she showed up earlier.

"She might well be holed up in a hotel close by so that she can gather the most dirt—or what she thinks of as dirt on us to be prepared to do battle." After seeing it was his brothers, all of them coming at the same time, he told Charles what Mac had told him.

"Battle? Yeah, I can see that. My wife will be close to me when she gets here and won't leave my side unless she has to. Mom will go to the kitchen to get away from her first thing. Dad will greet her but he'll not extend her any wishes. Not even if it's Christmas, a holiday that she hates, by the way. Let me see…the staff will wander in but won't serve her if she spouts off to them. After bringing it up to my parents a few times, she leaves them alone because Mom and Dad won't do anything to their staff for having the same opinion of her that they do. I think Mom would feel better if she were to just let all her hatred go about her, but she's a good person no matter what Grandmother does to her." He asked if he knew why she was coming. "Dad thinks money. So does Mom. Mac thinks it's because she's looking for us to invite her to stay with us. Last I heard, Grandmother was on an allowance, and it doesn't go all that far for the life that she leads. A very out-of-touch life with the way her money is gone in no time."

"That's very sad on her part, don't you think?" Charles said it wasn't to him as he was finished with her. "I'm glad to hear that. My parents have been warned not to take any shit from her either."

The doorbell rang again and that was when he noticed that there was a butler. Usually, when he'd come by, the Booths, one or both of them, would answer it. Today, he noticed that things were a little more formal, and he decided that he wasn't going to hold back if the woman gave him any shit.

Almost as if he'd orchestrated it, Milly came to stand between him and Charles. And Dani went to the kitchen. Or he supposed someplace in the back of the house. Something else occurred to him, too. They were having a cookout. Steaks, chicken, burgers and hot dogs. The table was set with festive paper plates with large bowls of potato salad and other sides. He was happy to see that there were steak knives as well. He thought this was part of the plan as well.

"What are all these people doing here, Charles? You know how I hate to come and visit you, and you have strangers all around." He told his mother that they weren't strangers to him, and she glared at him. "You know what I'm talking about. Tell them that we have important matters to attend to, and I won't have things said in front of them."

"Grandmother. Not that I care, really, but who let you out from under your rock? And no, we're not uninviting our friends over. Get over it." Mac, true to her word about her grandmother, looked at him with a wink. "Also, I want you to meet the man that I plan on marrying someday. He's an attorney. I know how much you detest that occupation."

"I've never known one of them to be honest. And you can bet that by the time I'm ready to leave, I'll have all the dirt on him, too. Even his family." Mac told her that they were all there if she wanted to tangle with them. "I don't like how you're speaking to me. Are you showing off to that supposed man of yours? It would be just like you to be a smart aleck when there are new people around."

"Really? You two are going to get married?" His brothers all wanted to give Mac a welcoming kiss. "This is awesome. I can't wait. Are you going to have kids right away? I want to be the best uncle if you do."

"There will be no children of that union, or I'll have something to say about that." Mac told her that she didn't care what she had to say. It was her body and her life. "We'll see about that. You there, you're his parents, I'm assuming? Why would you allow this to happen? She's already been jilted once at the altar. Do you have one bit of sense when it comes to what that will entail if they do ever marry? Damn it all, I'll have no trouble knocking some sense into you two as well."

"Did you have anything to do with that? I don't know why I think that but it only just occurred to me." She told him that, sadly, she'd not, but he'd done it all by himself. "But I've no doubt that you would have." He stood up, making sure that he towered over the elderly woman. "My name is Axel Hathaway. Yes, those are my parents and I would suggest that you take care when addressing them. Anyone of us will take you to task if you don't respect them when speaking to them."

"Who do you think you are talking to me that way?" He reminded her that he'd only just told her his name, then asked if she was having memory issues. "I do not. I remember everything. You'd do well to remember that in the future, young man. If there is one for you here. How did you meet her anyway? Why wasn't I informed about this supposed wedding?"

"Because you're not going to be invited for one thing. Secondly, I'm sure you understand that since no one here likes you that we don't care all that much for your opinion. Even if it was going to be nice." Axel eyed her shrewdly. "You talk to my parents like that again, and there will be no hole deep enough for you to hide in. You'll pay them the respect that they deserve, or you'll not speak to them at all. Do I make myself clear?"

His brothers all stood up and circled the old bitty. When she screamed that they were hurting her, he noticed that not one person stood up to defend her. If there had been a reason. She was a bully, and he didn't tolerate them any more than he would her. She wasn't worth it.

Dinner was called, and he was happy when Mac came to stand in line with him. They'd been asked their preference for dinner meat, and was happy that his steak was perfectly cooked. Mac had a chicken breast that was covered in sauce, and he decided that he would get himself a couple of bites to see if it tasted as good as it looked.

Hanna Booth didn't join them but sat in the living room by herself. From the living room, Charlie asked if she wanted her plate brought to her. He had a hot dog with her name on it, and she didn't bother answering her. When Dani looked at him, Axel could tell that she'd been crying.

"I'm sorry, Dani. I am." She said she wasn't upset but still laughing about what he'd said to her about his parents. "You need to say a few things like that as well. It might make you feel better about her coming to visit. As in, she won't come here to visit if she knows that she doesn't bother you anymore."

"You've given me such strength that I do believe that I can do that." She looked in the living room and then back at him. "You will have children with my daughter, won't you? I'd so love to have a little one or two running around."

"That will be up to Mac. Like she said, it's her body and her rules. I'm so glad that everyone isn't thinking that we've not known one another long enough to be talking about that but I do love her with all my heart." He handed her a small box that he'd picked up today before coming here. "What do you think? Do you think she'll like it? If not, I can get her something else, but it reminded me of her in some way."

"Oh, she'll love it. Are you going to do it today?" Axel told her that as soon as everyone was seated to eat, he was going to pop the question to her. "Good for you. That'll make the old goat pissed off more than anything. Oh, did you see that Chuck is avoiding her. I don't know what happened between the two of them but when she was here last, him being just a little baby, he would scream every time she came near him. I think she pinched him or something."

"She'll never do that again. Not so long as I'm around." When everyone was seated, he looked at Dani and kissed her on the cheek. Then, standing up, he turned to Mac. She looked a little confused until he got down on one knee. "Mackenize Booth, will you be my wife. Be my life. I love you so much now that it's hard to imagine my life without you being at my side. Or even in our bed in the morning."

"Yes. But I didn't think we were that far yet." He kissed her, and she laughed. "Well, I guess we are. Yes, I'll marry you, Axel Hathaway."

"What's going on in here? Get up off the floor, you moron. What do you think you're doing?" Axel told the old woman that he'd just proposed to Mac. "What a ridiculous name for a woman. And you'll take that back right now, you hear me? I told you, you'll not be getting married unless it's over my dead body. I told you to get up, and I'm not kidding around right now."

He stood up and looked at Ms. Booth. "I'm not taking anything back, and I plan on marrying Mac as soon as it can be arranged. If she wants, we'll have fifty kids, too. I have a nice big house that we can fill up over and over again." She put her hand over her heart and Axel couldn't hold back on his next question. "Is this the part where it's over your dead body now?"

"Why the nerve of you. I came here to talk

business with my son and you idiots are making it difficult. So there will be no lingering after that stupid meal. Once you're finished, I expect each of you to leave here to let me get to my business." When Dani stood up, she looked about as nervous as he'd been when proposing to Mac. "What do you think you're going to say to me. The only thing that I will allow you to open your mouth for will be to tell me that you've finally come to your senses and are leaving—"

"Get out." Hanna asked her what she'd said. "I said to get out. Get out of my house right now before I call the police. You've had your say about everything that didn't concern you. Now you're to get out of here before I toss you out on that fat ass of yours." She seemed to be gaining strength when Charlie put his hand over hers and laced his fingers with them. "You've been nothing but a royal pain in the backside since I married Charlie. Well, I've had enough. You'll no longer be welcome here for as long as this is my home with Charlie, nor will we seek out your opinions when it's none of your business. Get out now."

"I want to talk to my son, you harpy." Dani laughed and then told her that she wasn't getting any more money from them. Ms. Booth looked at her son. "What do you think your father would say if he were to hear the way everyone is speaking to me?"

"What would Dad say? He'd probably laugh at you and then tell me it's about time that I've gotten some balls." The hand to the heart again. "Yes, that's what I said, gotten some balls. And I do believe that my wife, my wonderful wife, told you to get out." Without looking at him, Charlie spoke to him. "Axel, if you'd not mind calling the police, I'd appreciate it."

"I'll take care of this, Charlie. I'm a cop. I'll gladly walk her out of your home." Penrod stood up and drew his gun out from under his shirt. "We can do this the easy way or the hard one — I'm hoping for the hard way — so you'd best be getting out of here before I take you in for simply being a fucking bitch." She left on her own two feet, telling them all that she'd be back.

When she was out the door on her own, everyone in the house, including the staff, laughed. It was a good laugh, too. However, he had a feeling this wasn't the last time they'd tangle with Hanna Booth. She was stupid, and stupid people didn't give up so easily.

Chapter 5

When her grandmother left, there was still some tension in the air but not like before. It was Axel's father that stood up, clapping his hands. Then the others joined him. Dad was slightly embarrassed, but it was her mom who seemed to understand what was going on right now. As soon as she went to the kitchen, each of them could hear her yelling '*yes*,' and Mac was prouder of her in that moment than she'd ever been all her life. It was her mom that got balls, not her day and she was thrilled beyond words.

After dinner and the clean-up was taken care of, they sat in the living room to talk. Milly wasn't feeling well, the baby, she said, and Charles and she went up to the bedroom they used when visiting. Chuck had fallen asleep hours ago and seemed just fine for laying on his dad's shoulder when they left the room. She hadn't realized it was so late until she heard the grandfather clock chiming that it was eleven o'clock. She had things to get going in the morning.

She did walk Axel out to his car. However, when the motion light went off, he pulled her into his arms and kissed her while pressing her against his car. Christ, he was hard as a stone, and his hands were all over her.

"I want you. I've never wanted to be buried so deep inside of a woman in all my life. I want to feel you come around me, over me. I want to feel your body milk mine until I'm so crazed with need that I can't see straight. I want to see you come Mac, taste you when you do."

Mac realized that he had taken them deeper into the shadows than they'd been before when he pressed her against the garage. It really was dark, but for the moonlight that was barely showing. When he slid her down his body, she could feel his cock pressing hard against her belly. Need, the need to feel him inside of her, raced through her. Axel gently pressed her back against the wall all the while kissing her, touching her.

Axel had his shirt unbuttoned from her before she realized it, and her bra pushed down over her swollen breasts. They were tender, so needy that she could barely stand to touch them. But what he was doing was sensual and gentle. And made her realize that it was because of him that she was like this, and she was thrilled that he was going to make her feel better in a few minutes.

"Mac, watch me suckle at your breast. I want to see your eyes glaze when you start to come. Watch me, baby." She did, not even caring how demanding his words were. "Oh, baby, I love you."

Mac leaned back and watched as he traced his tongue all along the areola, never touching the sensitive tip. His eyes never leaving hers, he flicked his tongue quickly over her nipple once, twice more before he covered it with his hot mouth and sucked.

Mac cried out from the feel of him rolling her nipple in his mouth and against the roof of the heat of his mouth. She felt him shift her around a bit, and then his hand was touching her between her legs through the material of her panties she moaned. Mac couldn't decide which felt better, his hand or his mouth, and soon it didn't matter. Her entire body was a live wire, waiting, waiting, and wanting something that she knew only he could give her.

"Please, I need…please help me, Axel." She nearly cried out again when he pulled his mouth away from her breast. She thought that he was stopping and silently begged him to not stop.

Axel was moving down her, down her body with his back to the opening in the driveway that if anyone were to come out, they'd only see him, not her too. It didn't take her long to figure out where he was going and what he was going to do. Before she could protest and tell him to stop, he had his mouth covering her clit, and she came apart, shattering into a million stars in the dark sky.

As he stood, she sat up and reached for him. She wanted to taste him as he had her. Fumbling with his buckle, she touched him as soon as he was free. His cock, hard and hot in her hands as she guided him to her mouth. Licking the tiny drop at the end of his shaft, she moaned at the taste.

Axel was hot and spicy, hard and smooth. Opening her mouth around him, he surged forward and bumped the back of her throat, causing her to gag slightly. He pulled back and cupped the back of her head, and gently showed her how to take him. Wrapping her hand around the inches she couldn't take in her mouth, she slid her hand up and down him.

"Mac, please…I'm so close, baby. I'm going to come." And she felt the first hot splash of him down the back of her throat. He rocked harder and harder as he came. Reaching between her own legs, still spread wide from him, she touched herself and came with him, moaning around his cock.

Mac fell back against the wall again, spent as he slowly leaned back against the wall of the garage again. She felt euphoric and happy. She laid her head on his chest and listened as his heart slowed. Her mind was all fuddled and still fuzzy from what they'd done.

"I love you, Axel. I think I always have." She felt him move beneath her. It was slight, but the way they were standing made it impossible for her not to feel it. Flushing with heat, she realized where they were and what they'd just done. Christ, she hoped the god there were no cameras here. Someone was going to get an eye full if there were.

"Mac, I'm sorry. I just can't believe what… it was fantastic but I…Christ, it was better than fantastic it was earthshattering and a bomb going off at the same time. I love you, honey." Then he laughed. "I bought us a mattress this morning, hoping that I could persuade you to come back to the house with me. I heard that the workers didn't work on Sundays. So I had this brilliant idea to woo you into my bedroom. I love—"

Mac cut him off before he said anything else. What he'd said already was enough to have her straightening out her clothing and then dragging him to the car he'd come in. "I'm sorry. I should go. I have things to do tomorrow, and I need to— I promise that I'll make this up to you."

"You leave without me, and I'm going to murder you." She got in on her side and waited for him to join her by getting under the steering wheel. "That was the best sex I've ever had, and I want more. More of it and certainly more of you."

"All right then." He had to get out of the car to adjust his own clothing. Once he was dressed again, she had to laugh. His pants were too small to come up over his still-hard erection. And he'd buttoned his shirt up wrong. It was off by two buttons. She couldn't stop laughing until he joined her. Then he stopped and put his head on the wheel. "I didn't get any protection. Damn it all to—" he looked at her. "I don't suppose you are?"

"No." She wanted to cry, and it looked as though he did as well. "We'll just be careful. And if a baby comes from us *'being careful,'* I will welcome it with open arms. We'll raise it, whatever she is together, right?"

"We'll marry as soon as I can get it arranged. Did you want a large wedding?" She told him perhaps later. "Good. I can do quick if you're all right with that, and we can get with our parents, if that's the route you want to go later on a large wedding." He grinned at her. "I'm all for whatever you want. I'm so in love with you that I could burst into song. Which, I'm telling you right now, you do not want to happen. My grandma told me once that I couldn't carry a tune in a bucket with the lid glued down."

They laughed and told stories to each other all the way to the house. Once there, she was feeling like they were going too far too fast, and she was chickening out. When Axel put his hand on her leg, she looked at him.

"Nothing needs to happen if you don't want it to. I swear on my mother's heart that I would never force you into anything or do anything to you that you don't want as much as I do." She let out a long breath. "Honey, we can't make this work if we don't talk to each other. All right? I mean, we're going to fast in this. I'm sometimes overwhelmed as well." He looked at the house that had a lot of lights around it because of the equipment and supplies lying around. "It's a lovely home, don't you think? When I saw it at the auction, all I could think about was that I wanted it. Then when I got it, paying about half of what I thought that I should have, it was like a dream come true. Then you came along and made it the best dream ever."

"You are a romantic, aren't you?" They laughed again. "I'm not sure what I want right now. I mean, I do want you, but having a baby because we couldn't wait just seems stupid on our part. I know that I'm the one that said it, but I'm thinking that it was lust talking, and we need to get our shit together before we bring a baby into this."

"I agree. Now that I can step back from it all." He grinned at her. "There are two bedrooms that are finished—as you more than likely know. Neither of them has any furniture in them but they do have nice mattresses in them. The one with the ensuite bathroom is yours. The master, which is still weeks away from finishing up, is close to where you'll be sleeping. I'll take the one at the other end of the hall."

They entered the house holding hands. He had had an alarm system put in and had to tell her the code twice before she got that it was the day that they met. She wasn't sure how much more in love she could be with this man but he was wearing her down about a lot of things. But were they going too fast? She didn't know if she wanted to be concerned with that right now. Mac was exhausted, and all she wanted to do was sleep.

As soon as she got her bed made up and was crawling into it, she felt every muscle in her body begin to relax. She didn't know if it had anything to do with the almost sex or the fact that she wasn't at home. But almost as soon as she closed her eyes, she was out.

Waking in the middle of the night, she didn't have any idea where she was. Getting up and staggering to the bathroom with only the moonlight as her light, she remembered that she was in Axel's home. Or theirs, as he was so fond of telling her. After washing her hands and getting herself back to her mattress, she wondered, not for the first time, if things were just too perfect in her life right now. Always waiting for the other shoe to drop, she laid back down in her bed and closed her eyes. Again, she was out almost as soon as she did that.

~*~

Axel was out getting them some breakfast when he heard from his dad. Glad now that he'd been able to get up early enough to talk to his dad, he told him about the stuff that was going on with Mac's grandmother.

"Hanna had been arrested because she'd hit an officer when he asked her to turn over her purse. In it, they were able to find two handguns as well as a couple of switchblades. Christ, son, she told the officer that she was going to kill off her son if he didn't pay her more money. As it is now, she gets about three grand every two weeks from the estate. Who couldn't live on six thousand dollars a month?" He asked him where she had been living. "In a retirement village. And I don't have to tell you that they're glad that she's gone. They've been trying to get rid of her for years. She just bullies her way into making them let her stay, and she wins. I can't imagine living with her all the time. She'd drive me batty."

"She's only been here for a few days and I would think that she's been driving everyone batty here now. I guess she's going to have to have a court date. Do you think that I'd be able to represent the family? I mean, I don't think it's a conflict of interest, but I'm not entirely sure, as Mac and I aren't officially married as yet." He pulled into the driveway only to be disappointed that the workers were already there. But he could see Mac talking to one of the men. "Dad, I think I need to rescue one of the workers. Mac looks like she's on the warpath right now."

Dad was laughing when he hung up. Getting out of the car, he made his way slowly to where Mac and the other man were. With his box of donuts in his hand and coffee in the other, he was ready to do whatever was needed to cool things down.

"She's making our lives more difficult. I wasn't hired by her, so I don't know who I should be listening to." When he looked at Mac, she shook her head just enough where he got it. The man didn't know that she was his boss, and for whatever reason, she didn't want him to know either. Not now, at any rate. "She said that she didn't want carpets in the bedroom. Who doesn't want carpets in the bedroom? And you said that too, but I talked it over with my wife, and she said that the floor would be too cold to get up and walk to the bathroom."

"I'll tell you what I told the foreman of his site, wear slippers. There will be no carpet put down on any of the rooms unless she or I say differently." He looked at Mac. "Can you think of any room that you'd want carpet in, love?"

"Not a single one. Like you said, wear slippers or socks if you don't want your feet to get cold." When she winked at him, taking one of the coffees, he opened the donut box when she held onto his as well. "Are those French crullers? For future reference, those are my favorite. Also, I don't like coffee. I can drink it, but I prefer iced tea. Thanks for getting this."

He was all right with ignoring the man while they talked about donuts. He was telling her that his favorite was apple fritters with a glass of cold milk when he was interrupted.

"Do I take up the carpets or not." He asked

him if he'd already laid the carpet. "Yeah, like I said, nobody in their right mind wants no carpet in the bedrooms." Nodding, Axel looked at Mac.

"You're fired." She put her hands on her hips as she continued. "You'll leave this job site on your own, or I call the police. You were specifically told not to put down carpet, and that is a purchase that neither one of us approved. Now—"

"You can't fire me." The man looked at him and twirled his finger around his ear like he was saying that Mac was crazy. That just pissed him off.

Handing the donuts and his coffee to Mac, he drew back and hit the man square in the nose. Watching him fall to the ground backwards made his entire day. When he looked at Mac, she looked as pissed off as he'd ever seen her. He asked her what he'd done.

"I wanted to hit him. You took my fun away." He told her that he could pick the man up so that she could do it, too. "No, it's all right. But next time, see if I want to knock the shit out of him first before you do it. You've knocked him out, and I wouldn't have done that with my punch. All right?"

"Yes, ma'am, I can do that." He called the police to have the foreman, Mr. Benny Courtright, arrested. He didn't know what kind of charges to press right now, but given time, he was sure that he could figure out something. As he was being hauled away, he found that the kitchen was nearly finished. The refrigerator had been delivered and was set up for them to use. Pulling out the milk and juice that was in it, it must have been Mac who had ordered some things, he was ready to face the day.

"I have two hearings today. One at eleven, the other at four. So I'm going to be late coming home. Will you be all right here? I know you will but I want to make sure that you don't need anything before I have to go." She told him not to forget to shop for protection. He told her that he'd already done that while getting breakfast. "Good. I'm still not sure, but it's good to know that if we are ready, then we'll have them." She stretched, and he could have taken her right there on the counter with all the men around. "I have some things I have to do today as well. The building downtown is coming along nicely. I did put carpet in the front room for clients. It was just too hard in the room and cold. I hope that's all right?"

"Yes. It's perfectly fine. I just have to make sure that I have it cleaned more often than they did at the other place I worked at. The lobby wasn't nearly as decorated as the offices were, and people rarely saw those for the conference rooms. I'm so glad that I'm getting out of that place." She asked him if they'd tried to talk him into coming back. "A couple of calls have come in but I've been ignoring them in favor of spending time with you. It's much more fun."

"Good. I have to tell my dad about firing Benny. I think he's the man that he's been having a little bit of trouble with for a while now. He'll either be happy or disappointed. I'm not in the mood for him being disappointed in me today. I'm on top of the world."

After getting a shower, he was going by his condo to change by nine-thirty. As soon as he got to the courthouse, he made arrangements for them to be married. He was serious when he told her that he would have a big wedding later if that was what she wanted. For now, they'd be married in the event that they had unprotected sex for whatever reason.

The first hearing that he had was a quick no-brainer. The man had robbed his neighbor of a great many packages over the last several months. After having his client put in cameras all around his home, he was able not only to catch him stealing his packages but also pissing in his azaleas. He'd been more upset about that than he'd been about the packages. The bush had been from his mother's home when she passed, and it was dying now. He was awarded more than he asked for, and Axel thought it was because most of the people on the panel had had the same thing happen to them at one time or another.

He was preparing for his second trial when he heard from Mac. Always glad to hear from her, she told him what was going on a the house and how much was being done to finish up both the living room and the dining room.

"Also, Jamie called. The man doing your furniture? He said that he has the table finished with the chairs, and he'll be bringing them tomorrow. Which is perfect timing as the dining room is ready to get set up. Also, did you know that my parents have the same table, a bit smaller than ours, and they've been trying to get rid of the two corner cabinets that go with it? You've been in their dining room. You know how crowded it can be." He asked her if she wanted them. "I do. I have a feeling that we're going to need the extra room for tableware and such, so that will be perfect. Jamie is going to give them a once-over so that he can make sure that they all match. Also, before I forget, I spoke to your brother Stamos. I had no idea that he was an electrical engineer—anyway, he's going to come over when the television arrives and hook it up with the stereo equipment that you already got for that room. I love the television, by the way and think that it'll look wonderful with the furniture surrounding it during the holidays and such."

"The office furniture has arrived too. It's been set aside until the office is taken care of. Did I mention that I'm having another office set up in the event that I want to take on a partner? I don't right now but if it comes down to it, I'll already have things set up." She told him he was good at thinking outside the box. "Thank you very much. Have you spoken to your dad yet about Benny?"

"He said his plan for the day was to have fired him and three other men who were working on your house. When Benny was taken away, I guess the other men walked off the site. Dad told me that he thought they were slowing down the progress at the house and was happy to see them gone. I believe him. Without them there as distractions, they were able to finish up those two larger rooms." He told her that it was beginning to feel like a home to him. "Me as well. When I was out there, I figured out that the pantry wasn't very large. I hope you don't mind but I'm having it expanded by taking out that closet that is in the dining room. I didn't know what that was for anyway."

"I think that it was a dish closet—at least that's what my mom called it. But with the two cabinets from your parents' house, we won't need it. And you do what you want to the house. I'm just happy not to be spending the rest of my life in a condo." She told him that she had an apartment somewhere but hadn't been in it for years. "Years? Sheesh, Mac, I do hope you didn't have any plants in there that needed attention."

Laughing, she told him that she'd been subletting it. "Good to know. I'm thinking about doing that with my condo. I don't want to have to go back there but the income from it would be a nice nest egg should we want to splurge on a cruise or something." She told him that she had to go but loved that idea. "Good, I'll make the arrangements to have it cleaned up and rented out. I love you."

"And I love you very much." Showing up at the courthouse a little before three, he was asked to sit in on a couple of other trials that were going on, not as an attorney but just as someone who could take some notes on the attorney who was working the cases. He didn't mind that, but he also told his buddy that he wasn't going to hold back when telling him what he observed, if anything.

"Good. I never expected anything less from you." He sat down in one of the many seats that were empty and watched the young woman as she spoke to the judge about her client. Whatever was going on, he thought that she was over stressed about it and needed to chill a bit. Her movements told him that she was either a stick in the mud or she was dealing with more stress than he'd thought. Listening in better, he heard her then.

"Yes, your honor, I know that he was put out on bail. If you remember, I was against that when the other attorney suggested it. Why he had any say in this is beyond me. But the very fact that he's not here shows the reason why he shouldn't have been allowed to be free." The judge asked her something, but he didn't hear it. "Threatened me? Yes. I've made it known to my boss that he's been threatening me with death since I took the case on. I don't have any way of making it so that he doesn't serve jail time with him admitting to the police that he'd killed the young child. His prints and DNA were all over the site. Again, I don't know why he was allotted bail when there was a murder involved."

"Give me a minute to look at this file, will you Ms. Author? It won't take but a few minutes of your time." She said that she had nothing but time for him. "Good girl. Also, I see Mr. Hathaway in the courtroom. Perhaps you can have a word or two with him concerning this other attorney. I believe he'll have some information that can help you stay safe, too."

Just as she reached him, putting out her hand to shake it, the back doors to the courtroom burst open, and gunshots were sprayed all over the room just as he pushed the woman to the floor and lay atop her.

"Debra? Where are you? Come out, come out from wherever you are?" Debra, he assumed, was beneath him, and she begged him not to let her die. It was her birthday today. The man, brandishing the gun, sprayed another round of shots into the room. Since he couldn't see anything from where he was, he had no idea how the man was still standing when he had a fucking gun. "Debra honey? Come out and play. For every minute I have to wait on you, I'm going to kill one of these people."

Then, just as another round of bullets took out the glass windows on his side of the courtroom, there was a single shot fired, and everything got eerily silent. He tried to sit up enough to see what was going on but was told not to move. He was able to move his body directly off Debra to allow her to breathe better.

It took nearly forty minutes for things to be straightened out enough that he was able to get up off the floor. He'd been allowed to move so that Debra could be questioned, but he never left her side. Holding his hand, she seemed to be dealing with what had happened much better than he thought that she would have under other circumstances.

"I did file charges against him just this morning. And the judge was…he killed him, didn't he? Judge Markus?" The officer said that the bailiff, as well as the court stenographer, were also killed. And there were several injured. "I'm so sorry. He would have killed me too if not for the fast thinking of Mr. Hathaway."

"I just reacted, that's all. When the doors opened, it was all I could think of was to keep us both safe."

The officer was a little green, but he was holding up well. It was more than likely his first murderer, as they had so very few in this town. In fact, other than the one that I have a hearing on next, it had been about a couple of decades since anyone had been murdered.

After another hour, he was finally able to see his family. They'd been called about two hours ago, and he was glad to see them. Especially Mac. Holding her while she sobbed into his chest about the fact that they'd only just got together, he told his parents that he was all right and didn't have to go to the hospital as the gun was never pointed in his direction.

Chapter 6

Bright and early the next morning, they were at the same courthouse that they'd been in yesterday. Only this time, things were much more quiet, and there wasn't anyone waving a gun around either. To look around, seeing the bullet holes in the walls and broken windows, made her heart beat a bit faster. Taking Axel's hand into her own, she wanted to take him home, wrap him up, and make sure he was safe for her at all time. As she was getting ready to go into the courtroom to be married, a young woman came up to her.

"I wanted to tell you that your husband saved my life yesterday." She said that they weren't married yet but were there to do it now. "Good for you. He is a good man, and he did really save me. Every time I think about being tossed to the floor by Axel, I want to find a dark corner and hide. He didn't hurt me, but the sounds going on around me and not knowing what was going on will haunt me forever. I will forever be grateful to him."

"I'm glad that both of you are all right. As soon as I was told about it, I had to get here and be with him. They wouldn't allow me to touch him until everything was cleared up." Mac felt her fear nearly get the better of her. Debra asked her if she was all right. "I am now. But yesterday, I was a mess. I know this is going to sound very strange, but would you like to stand up with me to get married?"

It was spur of the moment, and both of them seemed to be shocked by the question. When Debra told her that she'd be honored to do that for her after sharing her husband yesterday, Mac felt like it was the right thing to do. She didn't have any women friends at all and was happy that the two of them were getting along so well. Like they'd been friends forever.

The wedding ceremony was over in less time than it had taken them to get ready for it. She was happy now, and so loved the wedding ring that Axel had put on her finger. The diamond ring that he'd given her before was a perfect match to her blue eyes with the azures that circled it, and she loved that he'd given her two wedding bands. One for public, the other a safe one for working. She didn't want to lose a finger because she'd gotten married.

Debra was invited to have breakfast with them. It was at her parents' home, but she again felt like she just belonged there. After having as many little breakfast sandwiches as she could stuff into herself, she was ready for a long nap.

The cabinets had been removed just yesterday. That was what was going on at her parents' home when the police had called her. She didn't know if that was the norm around here but she didn't much care for having to hear about what had happened to Axel from the police. Yes, she told herself that he was fine, but what was going to happen the next time she kept asking herself.

"I'm all right." She said that her head knew that, but her heart didn't seem to care. "I understand that. It's the same with me. I didn't get anywhere at all hurt, but I find myself looking around for another shooter all the time."

"Don't tell me that." She then looked up at him. "All right, do tell me, but I don't want you hurt any more than what happened yesterday. You're mine and I'm going to keep you as healthy and as safe as I can. Can you deal with that?"

"I can. So long as you're there for me at the end of the day, I can handle about anything." Nodding, she told him again that she loved him, and he kissed her before telling her the same. As soon as they were seated in the living room, Debra not too far away, Axel's brothers came into the room with them to ask questions about what had happened. Since she didn't want to hear it again, Mac went to get herself some tea from the kitchen.

They were headed home when she remembered her grandmother. She had requested her to come and see her. She was sure that she'd not requested anything, but that was what the officer told her when he called. Mac liked that they were being more polite than her stupid grandmother was. They headed that way instead of going home.

The station house wasn't all that busy. She saw that the sheriff was sitting at his desk looking at files, and one of the only two officers on duty was doing a crossword puzzle. Funny enough, it was about policemen and she had a little giggle about that. She told Officer Emery that she was there to see her grandmother.

"She's in a right ripe mood, just so you

know. And she's more than likely starving on account of her not having her meal at breakfast or lunch today. We did bring it to her but she refused it on account of it wasn't what she had ordered. I tried to explain to her that we're not a restaurant, but she didn't want to hear it." He laughed a little nervously. "She only hears what she wants to hear, doesn't she?"

"That pretty much sums her up in a nutshell. She's been like that my whole life." Emery told her that he was sorry to hear that. He gathered up his keys, and she noticed too that he put his gun in his top drawer and then locked it with a key that he put in his front pocket. "Don't want to give her any ideas about shooting her way out of here, now do we."

Mac had a feeling that the young man was a great deal smarter and savvy than he was putting on. She noticed, too, that the crossword puzzle he'd been doing was in ink and that he'd filled out nearly all the little blocks. Yes, she thought to herself, this was a man going far in the world of police activity.

Her grandmother was sitting on a chair— not one that she thought would be all that comfy, but she didn't have any other choice. She didn't know where it had come from then noticed that all the rooms had a chair in the cells. However, they were all chained to the floor or wall. Good, she thought. They'd taken out another weapon for her to use.

"You certainly took your time coming here." She turned to leave but was called back. "Christ, you're just as bad as your mother. She was always a stupid cunt too."

"Talk about my mother like that again, and you can rot in hell for all I care. Tell me what you want so that I can consider it for about ten seconds before I tell you no. I'm busy, and this is my wedding night." She asked her on what authority did she think she could just get married. "Believe it or not, but I'm over twenty-one, and I don't answer to anyone anymore. What do you want?"

"I want out of here. And if you can't get your head out of your ass long enough to care about me, then I want you to find me a good attorney." She told her that she was married to a great attorney. "Good. Then he'll not charge me anything. Not that I would pay for it anyway, but it'll save you some cash. Also, I want more money than I've been getting from your father. He has a great deal of it, and I think that as his mother, I should be getting at least half, if not more, than he gets monthly."

"Is that all?" She asked her what she was talking about. "I mean, did you have any other demands while I'm here? I'm not going to do either of the ones you put out there, so if you have more than I can lump into my telling you to fuck off, then go for it now. I'm a busy woman, and I don't have time to come here when you're perfectly fine where you are. At least, that's what most of the town is saying. Oh, before I forget, you've been moved out of the village that you've been living in. They've put your things in storage for you to get when you want it. I'd hurry and make the arrangements for it if I were you. They're charging you by the day for the cost."

"What do you mean that I've been kicked out of that village? They can't run that place without me there. You tell them if one of my things, even my hair brush, has been moved, I'll own that place." Mac told her that she'd never paid for the place in the first place, so that was a no-brainer. "I have no idea what you're talking about. If your father would not have agreed to the things in that will, I'd not have to bother with...well, that's not true. I'd still come around to make sure that things are running the proper way."

She didn't say anything but she did glance around to see what Axel was doing. He was actually leaning against the wall with his cell phone out. It looked to her like he was playing a game. Good for him. He wasn't taking over. Not that she'd be mad at him if he did. She was just about ready to —

"Are you even listening to me? I demand an answer." She simply told her no. "No? That's not the answer that I want from you, and I believe you know it. I want what I want, Mackenzie, or so help me, god, you'll regret the day that you were born. Why they kept you is still a mystery to me."

"Perhaps, unlike you, they're good people. And they love me. Which surprises me that Dad would even know what that meant having you as his mother." She turned to leave, having enough of her grandmother for the rest of her life.

"You get back here. Do you hear me? I will not repeat myself." Over her shoulder, she told her that was good, it was boring anyway. "Mackenzie Booth, you're going to regret this."

"You keep telling yourself that." She was

out in the sunlight before she could remember if they'd appeared there. Axel was holding her, and she felt like she could lean on him forever, and he'd never stop being all that she needed in the world. "I don't want to ever go back in there to talk to her again."

"I'll take care of her from now on if that's all right with you. Your dad told me the same thing. That he didn't want to have to deal with her anymore. She's very caustic, isn't she? Demanding too. I know that I'm not telling you something that you don't already know, but damn, she's a fucking bitch. How on earth did your dad turn out to be such a good man?" She told him what she knew. "So your grandda pretty much raised him and made him into the man he is today. Then how did he put up with that woman? I'm betting that she trapped him somehow."

"She did. She said that he was the father of her child. My dad wasn't my grandda's son. But he didn't care once he was born. I guess not only did he shower him with love and compassion, but he also showed him how to run an already successful business as well. Booth Reno was his baby when he was alive. He was very good at investing, too. When he passed away, he left everything to my dad. And if he were to give his mother, my grandmother, any more than she was getting now, he'd lose it all. But I don't think that was ever a thought in his head to give her anything more than she was getting anyway."

Hand in hand, they walked to the car. It was a beautiful night despite grandmother's visit, but right now, she was having a lovely evening with her most favorite person in the world. They decided that they'd get ice cream before their dinner, and she was all right with that. Ice cream was better than a full belly of carbs any day of the week.

She got her favorite and made fun of Axel because he got vanilla. She liked it, too, the flavor went with all sorts of toppings that she loved. Hot fudge, sprinkles, and several cherries on the top. And not to forget the best topping, whipped cream too.

"I want to take you home and make love to you for the rest of the evening." She told him that she would love that. "Good. Seeing you eat your ice cream makes my cock hard, and my heart beat a bit faster. How about we eat these on the way home so we'll be that much closer to having a great night of sex with lots of climaxes?"

"Or we could just toss these and get there faster by walking. I'm sure that no one will mind us leaving the car here for the night." He told her that he loved the way that her thought process worked. "Thank you. I've been thinking of this night for my whole life it seems."

After throwing away their cones into the trash, they decided not to take the chance of leaving the car in the courthouse lot. Instead, they pulled off on the short drive a couple of times and necked a bit. She'd never done that as a teenager and found that it was quite exhilarating.

~*~

Almost as soon as they were in the house, they were running up the stairs laughing. Axel was thrilled now that he'd put together the bed that he'd gotten today and put the mattress on it. It was larger than he'd remembered, and he was glad for it.

Releasing her hands, he cupped her ass again and picked her up. Her legs wrapped around his hips, and her arms encircled his neck. Axel covered her mouth with his and ate at her as he moved forward toward the wall across from the door to their room. Riding her up and down his cock, he pressed harder into her when her back touched the wall. Using it as leverage, he pulled her shirt from her jeans and ran his hands under to touch her bare skin. Everything about her was hot. Her sweet smelling breath to her skin everywhere he touched her.

Heat and soft skin, his hands could not stop touching her. Lifting his hands higher, Axel cupped her breasts and moaned at the weight of them in his palms. Using his thumbs, he slid under her bra and rubbed her hard nipples.

Need to taste them had him tear from her mouth and pull one into his mouth through the shirt and bra and bite. Her hiss of approval gave him all the encouragement he needed, and he started working at the buttons while he nuzzled at her full breast and pulled at the other nipple with his thumb and finger.

"I need to taste you. I want to suckle at your breast and taste you. Help me, baby." She started pulling off her clothing and he was helping. They kept fumbling over one another until she seemed to have enough.

She smacked his hands away and lifted her blouse up and unclasping the closure in the front of her lacy blue bra. No wonder he couldn't undo it. He'd not thought of it being in the front. As soon as it was open, he pushed the edges open and rubbed his nose over the hard peak, then took it deep into his mouth. She was rocking hard against him, and with every push from the wall into his body, he countered with a rock back into her. When he bit down on her nipple, she moaned and growled at him.

"Please, Axel. If you don't stop, I'm going to come right now. And you did remember that we hired a cook last week and she's right down stairs. You have to stop now before it's too late."

"It's already too late. Come for me, baby. Come right now. I'll catch you. I want to feel you come."

He rocked harder, and with his free hand, he reached between them and pressed his thumb against her clit hard and then harder still. When her body stiffened, and he felt her start to shatter around him, he covered her mouth with his and captured her screams.

Axel kept rocking into her heat. His cock

ached to be released and driven into her hard and fast. He held her as she came down from her release, as her body shuttered and shivered at the amount of power that had come with it. Axel held her as her body became relaxed, sated, and limp against him. When she rested her head on his shoulder, he let her legs fall to the floor, but he did not let go of her. Soon, her breathing became normal, and with it, her eyes looked directly into his, and he could feel her love for him right then. He leaned back and pulled her body to his again.

Taking her to the bed, he laid her gently on it. It was far from what he was feeling, and he was trying his best not to hurt her in any way. Christ, but he was aching to come. On her or over her or inside of her, he simply didn't care at this point. He rocked into her again, and it had her stiffening up as she started to come once again.

"That's it, baby. Don't hold back. Come when you feel it, come and scream for me. I love to watch you peak, your body shudders over mine, and I feel you. Feel you everywhere."

He moved down her body. When he forced her legs to let him go, she whimpered and tried to pull him back, but he kissed her hard and brought his hand to her mound.

"I'm going to eat you here, Mac. I'm going to lick you and taste you until you can't stand it anymore. I'm going to drink you as you come, as you fill me. Then I'm going to drive my cock hard into you. Deep and fast, and fuck you until neither of us can move."

When he moved this time, she grabbed the sheet beneath her. She could feel her pussy flutter and gush. Need curled inside of her, and she had a hard time holding the part of her back that terrified her more than anything.

Axel nuzzled her mound, and when she felt him move the bit of lace from her, she tried to close her legs to him. It wasn't really that she was trying to stop him just something that he thought was instinct to her. He pressed her open and braced her with his shoulders as he ran his finger along her slit, gathering her cream as he went.

"Watch me, Mac. I want you to see me lick your cream from my fingers." He brought his fingers to his mouth and suckled each one, savoring the taste. "Oh honey, you taste better than I thought, baby. Like honey and peaches."

When his finger slid into her she did not

stop watching him, seeing the look of rapture on his face. Struggling now to hold on, he knew she was loving what he was doing to her and he loved it when she was so vocal with her releases.

"I want you, Mac. All of you. Please, help me get ready for you." Axel reached for the condoms that he'd gotten and fumbled around with it for a few seconds as he was too hard, it seemed, for them to fit. Once he had to use a second one, the other burst when he tried to pull it down over himself. He nearly wept with relief when he was about as covered as a man could be with one of the things.

He pumped his finger into her, over and over, and when he added a second one, he lowered his head and slid his tongue into her. Moving more between her legs, he worried her clit with his tongue as he fucked her with his fingers. The coil of need tightened around him so tightly that he was hurting badly when all he wanted to do was fuck his pretty little wife.

Every time she got close, he would pull back and not touch her clit until the need to come lowered a bit. But it was getting harder and longer to slow down. Wrapping her hand into his hair, she tried to get him to where she wanted, but he was stronger and did what he wanted. Begging only made him chuckle, and when she thought she was going to have to hurt him, he gave her what she wanted.

He bit her clit hard and then suckled it into his mouth as he'd done her nipples; she knew it was too much. Her control snapped, and so did her hold. She wanted to come with him deep inside of her, fucking her like she wanted.

Her world froze for a second then everything in her seemed to shatter. He could hear her screaming. It ripped from her throat, no doubt leaving it raw and sore. Every nerve, every cell in her body exploded as his did. Stars, bright and colorful, burst behind his closed eyes. Muscles contracted, her body expanded, and when she felt Axel move over her and his cock slide into her, she screamed again, another climax taking her breath away. Her body tightened around him, pushing his cock deeper into her. Mac heard him growl, heard him speak but she was beyond knowing what he said. As soon as he was close enough to touch, she wrapped herself around him and let go.

It was nearly overwhelming, nearly consumed him, the love that he had for her. Even as he rolled to his side, taking her with him, he knew that he'd never have another woman in his life but her. Moving so that she had more room on the bed, he didn't move for a few minutes before having to get up and go to the bathroom to dispose of the condom.

It was then that he realized that the sucker had broken, and they'd just had unprotected sex. Washing up, he headed back to bed to tell her, but she was snoring softly. Turning her gently to her side, he was happy that she curled around him in her need for more comfort.

Closing his eyes, he was sure that he was asleep before his body was fully relaxed. His entire body was achy but not really sore. When she got up to use the bathroom, he was simply too exhausted to tell her about the condom. He didn't care if they'd made a child between them. But it was her body and her choice. He only hoped that she'd believe him when he told her how sorry he was.

"Tell me." He looked at her with one eye. "Tell me what has you grumbling. Something about me being pissed off. I don't know if you noticed this or not, but I'm too relaxed to be pissed about anything right now. So? What happened?"

"The condom broke." She lay there for several minutes, longer than he thought was necessary, before she started to laugh. He didn't know what she was thinking about, but he was nervous that he might well have broken her during their lovemaking. "Can you tell me what's so funny? I'd like a laugh about now, too."

"For all our prep, we still had unprotected sex." She rolled over and looked at him as they lay face to face. "I love you, Axel. So very much. And if we made a baby today, I'm thrilled beyond words. I'm sure that your family will be as well. Don't you think?"

"They'll start buying things to spoil their first grandchild as soon as we tell them. I can see my mom knitting too, some kind of booties. Do babies still wear them? I don't care. They'll both, hell, they'll all be so happy that they'll treat you with kid gloves." She told him that she'd only put up with that once before she had to put her foot down. "Yeah, I don't see you as liking being pampered too much. You should warn them, however, before you go popping them in the head."

"Maybe." She rolled to her other side and

backed her body into his so that they were back to chest. "I'll not let Kahana give me the test when I know something. He strikes me as someone who wouldn't be able to hold a secret. Maybe not. I'll have to wait and see. How do you feel about us having a baby after only just getting married?"

For an answer, he put his hand on her flat belly. When she put her hand over his, he smiled into her neck and told her just how much he loved her. It was all he could have hoped for in a wife and maybe a family. She was the best thing that had ever happened to him.

It was nearly midnight when he woke up. He was suddenly famished and decided to go to the kitchen to whip them up something quick to eat. Axel was surprised to find a dozen or so little half sandwiches in there with plastic over them. Also there was fresh tea as well as chips that were laid out on the counter for them. Taking it up, he wasn't surprised to find Mac pulling on a robe to join him.

They ate in the bed. Not the best possible place but it worked for the two of them. When he had unearthed some fruit, mostly grapes, on the counter, too, he'd brought them up and was feeding them to Mac as she told him what was on her list for the day.

"The building downtown is nearly finished up but for the carpet that you wanted in the lobby. I can't pick that out for you—I guess I could, but I won't be working there when it's finished, so I have no say in the way it looks. My mom used to be an interior decorator when I was a kid and she told me that if you don't want carpet, she can soften up the room with some things that will make it look really homey. I told her that I'd ask you." He told her that would be wonderful as he bit into his third roast beef sandwich. "Good. I thought you'd say that, but I'll tell her tomorrow."

"I'm done with the other firm. They have been trying to get me to come back but I'm done with working for someone else. I'm actually excited to be working for myself. And like I said earlier, if I need more help, I can take on a partner, but I'm not seeing that happening." She said that her dad was hinting about retiring again. "How many times has he done that? I'm assuming a few times. Will he turn it over to you?"

"I'm not sure that I want it now. Not with having you in my life. I mean, I'll take it as my own, but I won't be working the jobs anymore unless the help is needed. I want to be here with you." He told her that he could understand that, but if it was money, he could support them both without any trouble at all. "No, I'd have to do something. I can't be a rich attorney's wife and not have a job. Besides, I have money too. Owning this business for as long as we have, we're not hurting for money at all. I even have a nice retirement plan thanks mostly to my mom looking into that when I first started working for my dad. I have a fat 401K too."

"As do I. But I'm not looking to retire just yet. Like you, I'd need to have a job or something to do that wouldn't get me into trouble by being idle." She told him that she was glad to hear that. "Good, then that's settled. Now that I'm full, I'm exhausted again. How about I clean off this stuff, and we get some sleep. Tomorrow will come earlier than we would want it to."

After she fell asleep, he put all the things that they'd used on the dresser. Walking back to the bed, he felt like a new man when he thought about Mac heavy with their child. Life, he thought, couldn't get any better than it was right now.

Chapter 7

Debra had everything packed that she was going to take with her. The rest was going to go to a charity place, and even that wasn't very much. Looking around the room once more, she was almost giddy with the change in her life. Her uncle had given her an easy way out of her debt as well as clearing up all the student debt that she still had from law school. It wasn't going to be all bread and honey, as her grandma used to say.

Working with her uncle was going to be difficult. He may well have offered her the law firm, but he was the type of man who didn't care for a working woman and, especially, one who was as educated as she was. But he'd offered, and now—

The phone ringing had her taking in a deep breath and rubbing her chest for the hundredth time today. Picking up her cell phone, her number not known to that many people, showed a recent picture of her uncle and she made herself have a bright smile when she said hello.

"Who is this?" She told the man on the other end of the line her name and then did the same for him. "I'm your cousin, Phillip Author." He paused long enough for her to no doubt be impressed that he'd taken the time to call her. "My grandda passed away two days ago. Getting into his phone was the only way that I knew of to contact you. There isn't any reason for you to come home for the funeral or will reading. You're not mentioned in it, and I'm having the old bastard cremated."

"I know for a fact that I'm mentioned in the will, Phil." He told her that his name was Phillip. "So? Also, you might want to remember that he's my uncle as well. He and I had an arrangement."

"Yeah, about that. I'm taking it. And everything else the old bastard had." She asked him if he suddenly had a law degree. "I don't need to have a law degree to run the firm. I just need money. And I'm also getting all of that, too. You know how he was about you working. And if you call me Phil once more, I'm going to sue your ass for defining my character."

"It's defamation, you idiot. And you do need

a law degree to own a law firm. Also be a licensed attorney in order to run one. Don't you ever look things up before you go spouting off things you are wrong about? And I will be there. Seeing you get your comeuppance will make it worthwhile." She disliked Phil with as much passion as he did her, apparently.

She felt her panic get the better of her and had to sit down. Lucky for her, there was a chair close by or there was no telling where she might have ended up. Lying her head on her table, she groaned when someone knocked — more like they pounded on her door to her apartment. She opened the door to see not just one of the Hathaway men but three of them. They sat on the couch that was going out to wait on her and her call.

Her hand gripped the phone tighter. He was getting on her last nerve. "Phil, you can't just think that I'm going to make your word for not being in the will. Uncle promised me that I could take over his firm when he retired. And I would assume that the same thing holds true because he's passed on." She was handed a phone that had a message on it to tell him what the firm was that her uncle used. After typing it on the little screen, she remembered that this brother was Axel, the attorney. "I'm going to be there as soon as I make a few calls. And if you're trying to keep me from showing up when I'm mentioned in the will, they won't be able to execute anything without all parties there."

Debra wanted to hang up on her cousin, but she was afraid that he was telling her the truth. It would be just like her uncle to say one thing and then do something entirely different. But she did remember just then that she had it in writing from him, she just needed to remember where she'd put it. Going through the few law books that she had, she found it and handed it to Axel. Nodding his thanks, she decided that she was going to be sick if she didn't get off the phone with her fucking bastard of a cousin.

Putting the phone on her table, she asked the doctor one…she couldn't remember his name for the life of herself, why they were there. He looked at Axel but didn't answer her.

"Well, if you don't know, then I think that it's time that you moved on. I have a sort of crisis going on here, and I have nothing to entertain anyone with." She'd not cared for this brother.

She found him to be arrogant and sort of

selfish. When going to the door to shoo them out, he smiled at her, and she wanted to bash his head in. Taking a step back, she hoped that they'd just leave on their own so that she could think. She needed to know what this was going to mean for her if she wasn't in the will.

"Mac sent us to help you move some of your things out to your car or whatever you're going home in." She liked Mac very much but couldn't think over the now-pounding headache that she was getting. "Mac seemed to think that you weren't taking all that much, but we should be nice to you because she said she'd beat our asses if we weren't. I'd like to think that I'm—what's the matter with you? Are you sick?"

Instead of answering him, she put her hand over her mouth and ran to the bathroom. There was only a small amount of things in the little room, but it was enough for her to rinse out her mouth after throwing up everything that she had for breakfast. She came out of her bathroom to find Kahana, that was his name, standing near the door. Glaring at him, the best that she could do with her stomach churning up, she asked him again when he was leaving.

"You're stressed out." She just glared at him. "Listen, I'm trying to be helpful to you." She told him that she wouldn't tell Mac about his bedside manner if she ever talked to her again. "I don't think she got that memo. The way she's talking— come sit down before you pass out. You're as white as a ghost."

This time, she didn't argue with him about how she looked or felt. That feeling in her chest, like she was being squeezed to death, was back. Putting her hand over her chest, she nearly fell over the back of the couch to sit down when she simply blacked out.

When she woke up, she was not just in her home but she was on a gurney that had somehow appeared while she was out. Trying to sit up, it was Kahana who told her to lie still. No, please. No, will you lie down? Just stay the hell down. She tried once more when he put his hand on her chest and got into her face.

"You're having a heart attack. How long have you been feeling this way?" She told him that it was stress and that the hospital told her that she wasn't to take up their time when indigestion was what she had. "It's not indigestion. You are having

a heart attack. Just lie still and let us take you to—
do you know who told you that you weren't ill?"

"The head nurse from the third shift. Why? Are you going to yell at her as well?" When he growled at her like he was some damned dog, she started feeling the pressure again. "She told me that I was wasting resources in the emergency department and that I should just stay home. They wouldn't even check me out the last time I was there but told me to go home and take an antacid." She looked up at him. "Am I really having a heart attack?"

"Yes, you really are. It's a small one but enough to cause some damage to your heart if not treated properly. Now, hush." When she felt something pinch at her arm, the pain in her chest eased up. It didn't go away, not entirely, but she did feel less in pain than before. "I know that nurse. I'm assuming that you were in there at the end of her shift. Other people have complained about her before. How many times in the last week have you been to the emergency department?"

"Ten times in five days. It was making me sick; it was so bad." An IV was in her arm, and she looked at it like she'd never seen one before. "My uncle is a bastard, and now I have no home, no place to sleep, and I won't be able to ever pay off my student loans. I was…I don't remember what I was doing." She could barely understand herself. Her words were like she'd been on a long drunk.

Even though she'd felt better a few minutes ago, she wasn't now. The pressure was building up, and before she could complain, she heard a loud beeping noise. Not caring all that much about what was going off, Debra passed out again.

~*~

Kahana kept up with the compressions while doing CPR on the woman. He was about as pissed as he'd been in a while and had to make sure that he wasn't pushing too hard on her small chest. Trading off with one of the medics that had come on the ambulances, he watched as the paddles were being warmed up to shock Debra again. They'd lost her three times already.

The very fact that she could speak made him think that she was in better health than he was. When he'd been in college, they had simulated a heart attack for the med students so that he'd know what they were dealing with. After the first trial, he was ready to give in. She had had three yet terribly small heart failures in a row and still had the energy to speak to him.

As soon as the ambulance pulled up in front of the ED doors, he was off the thing and barking orders. His temper over Debra being mistreated pissed him off, and he knew that he was taking it out on the others around him. As soon as she was hooked up to a monitor, he knew that if he'd not been there when she'd fallen, Debra Author would be dead. As it was now, it was touch and go.

With the right type of meds and someone monitoring her, she was going to be all right if she could make it past the next twenty-four hours. His head was hurting with his anger, and he had to take several deep breaths before he could call Mac and then his parents. Dad would calm him like no one else did, and he needed him nearby. Pulling Debra's hand up to feel her pulse, he kept holding onto her hand when she seemed to have the same effect on him that his father did. Calming of his mind and stress.

After telling his dad and mom what was going on, he was glad that Axel had told his wife. Mom was upset more than he thought necessary for a woman they barely knew, but he knew enough to keep his mouth shut when she asked him if there was any family.

"I don't know, to be honest. When we got to the apartment, she was already speaking to someone. She made it sound as if someone had died and that her cousin, I didn't catch his name, was telling her that she had nothing to do with the person who had passed on." Stretching his neck now that he was calmer, he told them what had happened in the ED when she'd come in the last time. "She actually told a person having a heart attack to go home and not return. I know we're only getting one side of the story, but Christ, even if she came in and they sent her on her way without checking her, the hospital would be looking at a big lawsuit. And if she had died...I don't even want to think about the repercussions of what that might have done."

"What do you have planned for this? You said that you know the nurse. Are you planning to report her?" Kahana told him that he was. If for no other reason than for her to learn what the consequences of her actions had happened. "You're right. And I'll back you as a board member. But I will tell you that this is not the first time her name has run across my desk as a board member. I hate to say this but I'm betting that they fire her for this one. And more than likely serve some serious jail time. Not to mention her losing her nurse status."

"Good." He didn't like to see anyone lose their job, but this woman could have killed Debra by being tired at the end of her shift or even, as he thought, thinking that Debra was faking her symptoms. "I'm going to be here awhile to make sure that she's treated. I think that Axel is looking into something for her about the death I was telling you about. Dad, I just don't understand people. Do you?"

"Not for a very long time, son. I'll come by later and bring you something to eat. You take good care of that girl. Your mom and Mac got along great with her." He told his dad that he would and thanked him for bringing him in something to eat. It was going to be a long night, and once Debra was put in the cardiac unit, he did rest a bit better.

Pulling up Debra's file told him several things at once. She'd been in the ED six times, but when she'd been told to go home, the nurse on duty said that she'd left against medical advice. An AMA was a way for her to get out of not treating her. And he no more believed that she'd left that way on her own. He was still looking over the files in Debra's room when she woke up.

"How are you doing?" She looked at him, confused. "It's Doctor Hathaway, Kahana. I was the one that brought you in here by ambulance." She struggled to speak, and he told her not to stress herself out.

"Where?" He told her where she was and why. After having the nurse check her blood pressure, he wasn't happy with how high it was. "Hurt."

"I'm sure you do." He checked her for numbness as well as a droopy left side. When she seemed to be better than she was at her home, he sat down in the chair that was next to her bed. "Do you remember talking to me at your apartment?"

She started to shake her head and stopped when it was obvious that it hurt too badly. He again told her to rest and that there wasn't anything she could do right now that would help her. Just for her to relax.

"I have a headache." He told her that was more than likely a side effect of the meds that she'd been given. Mostly the nitroglycerin. "You said that I'd had a heart attack. How do you know?"

He didn't care to be questioned about what he'd said or done while working but he did tell her that he'd seen her type of symptoms before. Then he told her about her dying several times, and without having a crash cart nearby, she wouldn't have made it. Nodding, Debra closed her eyes.

Kahana knew that the next time she woke up, he'd have to tell her again what had happened. This was the second time that she'd woke, and he'd had to remember everything that he needed to tell her without getting her upset again. She was doing much better than he thought that someone might have been doing while in the condition that she was currently in.

After pulling up the file on Ronda West, acting head nurse for the third shift ED department, he was also able to pull up her disciplinary file as well thanks to his dad for giving him access. As early as five days ago, she'd been written up for mishandling of medications. It was the fifth such one in her file. There were others, too, that were fairly new. One that she'd been very rude to a staff member and also once to someone who had come in for help. She'd sent that person home as well.

It worried him that she was getting away with so much until he got to the back of her file. The personal file. He called his dad back.

"Ronda West is Ben Wests wife." Dad told him that he'd not known that. "I'm betting that a great many people didn't know that. Her wage isn't in here, but she is being paid as much as a surgeon tier two it says here in her file. That's about as much as I make now. Something is fishy with this, and I don't know who to turn to about it."

"It's a bet that Ben knows what's going on. It is his wife...hang on a moment, son. I want to ask your mom something." He looked over at Debra and watched as the machine took her blood pressure. It was down a great deal than what it had been when she'd been at her home. Even coming into the hospital, it was down. He was glad for it. He didn't want anything to happen to her when she'd been a victim of someone in the medical field. "They're divorced. Ben and Ronda divorced about a year ago now, your mom told me. Tell me how far those disciplinary write-ups are."

He told his dad. "I thought so. About the time he started having an affair with his secretary, and Ronda found out. I'm betting that he's going to stay married to her so that there isn't this huge mess of a scandal about his job being head of surgery. He's keeping her quiet by letting her get by with...do you suppose he's keeping track of things hoping that someone else gets into her records and he's off the hook?" He told his dad that it made sense. "Yes, I'm betting that's just what is going on. Christ, son, the shit is going to hit the fan for all of them once this gets out. And I know just the place to let it happen, too. I have a buddy at the newspaper who would love a scandal like this one to add his name to."

He loved the way his father's mind worked. No one in his family would be in the article, and the woman and her ex-husband would get what they had coming to them. As soon as he was able to tell his dad about the other things in the file, he hung up and felt better about it.

Still going through the file, he found other things that he'd bet would help the man that his dad knew. He'd never been as proud of his parents as he was right now. And the great part of it was, it wouldn't come back to bite any of them in the ass. That he loved more than anything.

He was glad that he was with Debra all night. It made him feel better knowing firsthand that she hadn't had any more episodes like the one she'd had at home. Every time he thought about it, if she'd been alone, it made him all the more angry about the way that West, both of them, had gotten away with things.

When she looked at him, he decided to wait until she spoke. Her speech wasn't slurred, and her facial muscles seemed to be intact. Telling her for the fourth time what had happened, she didn't fall asleep right away but asked if she could have a drink of water. Her mouth was dry.

"I can give you some ice chips. You'll like them better anyway. Also, as I said before, don't let your pain overwhelm you. If you hurt then take something now rather than letting it get the better of you." She nodded and closed her eyes. He thought that she'd gone back to sleep when she spoke again.

"I had a heart attack. What happens to me now?" He asked her what she meant. "I mean, do I have something that I'm going to have to deal with for the rest of my life? Will I have to, I don't know, learn some things that I've known most of my life.

To be honest with her, I don't feel too bad right now, and I think this is the first time in longer than I can remember that I didn't feel like my head was going to explode and my heart to be pounding out of my chest. What happens to me now?"

"You've had two mild heart attacks. Not to say they weren't serious, but they were mild enough to not have you have paralysis to your body. You seem to have your memories intact as well." She asked him about medications. "Yes, you'll be on a few that I would like for you to take for the rest of your life. But you're young and healthy, so I don't see you having any more ill effects from this. You will have to deal with stress a little better. Other than that, I think you'll have a long life so long, as I said, you take care of yourself."

She looked at him. "I had to go home. I mean, I have nothing here, and since I more than likely didn't get to go home, I've lost everything." Kahana told her that his brother and father took care of things for her. "I don't know what that means. How did they take care of me not being there for the reading of the will."

"I don't know all the particulars but Axel has your phone and has been to Tennessee and back for you. The will that was being read isn't the original, it was figured out but a forged one that Phillip Author made taking you out of the will. Apparently, he showed up with his will and expected since he was the one who was getting everything in his will, no one would question him. By the way, he's in jail right now."

She closed her eyes again before speaking. "Thank him for that. I don't know what I'm going to do with it. I'm thinking that being an attorney will be more stress than I can handle anytime soon. And I'd still have to deal with Phil—a name he hates, by the way." Kahana laughed. "He's worse than you are when it comes to arrogancy. You are, you know that, don't you?"

"I do. It's saved me a great deal of time and energy when I'm dealing with idiots. Speaking of which, while you were getting some beauty rest, not that you need it, it's coming out soon about Ronda West and her ex-husband." He filled her in on what he knew. "There is going to be a huge article written in the newspaper which will more than likely be picked up all over the country if not the world. It's a small wonder that you survived on what happened to you. Axel is hoping that you'll press charges since you nearly died because of the woman."

"She did make me feel stupid. That's why I didn't go back after that but tried to deal with it on my own. It didn't work all that well...if they thought that I was faking my heart issues, then why did I get some nitro to use at home. It helped, by the way, but didn't take all the pain away." He told her what he knew about that. "So they were trying to cover their asses by giving me something so that I'd not come back. That's pretty shitty if you ask me."

"Yes, I agree with you." He took her blood pressure when he realized that she'd not been hooked back up to it when she'd been brought back from her CAT scan. So far, he told her she didn't show any signs of a lot of damage, and he hoped for the best outcome for her. "As I said, you'll need to watch some things. You'll have a list before you go home. Also, medications as well. There are a few that you'll need to take just to keep this from happening again. And you'll also need to get you one of those bracelets to tell that you have...never mind. We'll go over that later. Do you still want something to drink? I have some crushed ice for you if you wish."

He fed her several spoons of the cold ice and watched the monitor while she sat up better in the bed. So far, she was looking good, but he also knew that things could turn for her in a second's notice. He kept telling himself that he should just let the doctors who knew more than he did about heart issues take over as he was only a general practitioner.

By the time he was ready to go home, she was sitting in a chair enjoying the sunlight. He'd never met anyone that loved the sun shining as much as he did and was glad to be able to leave her in the capable hands of the intensive care unit or ICU. He was about as exhausted as he'd been when doing rounds in college.

Like his brothers, he didn't have a house. Axel did, but he didn't want all that space bogging him down. The condo that he'd been living in since they'd been kicked out of their home by their parents—he loved that they did that too—he'd been staying in a condo that was close to the hospital. Now, he didn't want that. He wanted to be able to have a little distance between him and his place of work.

Taking a shower, something that he'd not been able to get while staying with Debra, he fell into his bed after tossing his towel near to the laundry basket. Being clean and feeling relaxed, he fell into bed nude and closed his eyes. Getting up one more time, he called the service and took himself off of being on call but did tell the woman that if Debra Author were to call for him, then to put her through. He didn't know why he'd done that and was trying his best not to look too deeply into it.

Sleep wasn't coming on as well as he hoped it would. Finally, after tossing and turning for about an hour, he got up and dressed. That damned woman was on his mind, and he didn't care for Debra invading his rest time. After several more tries to get her out of his head, he finally went to his office to have a little bit of filing and paperwork done that he'd been putting off since he'd met the woman.

Kahana was on his second cup of tea when he was just finishing up his last file. It felt really good to have his desk cleaned away and even more satisfying to be able to have all the backlog of notes in files finished off as well. He even had time to run a vacuum and a duster over the furniture in the lobby.

He didn't exactly care for the office he was working in, he just realized. He'd been working out of it since he graduated from college. It was a place that he took so he'd have a place to work. It turned into, quite by accident, the place that he saw his patients in as well. It was old and had crappy furniture in it that he was ashamed to now realize that people might judge him by what they saw in the room. Getting back on his computer, it took him nearly five hours to not just arrange to have the carpets pulled up but the entire building revamped so that he could be proud of working here. And his new sister-in-law was going to give him a great discount on the job too.

His phone ringing startled him, and he nearly didn't answer it. It was his dad, and he said that he was going to see Debra about the lawsuit that was coming up against the hospital.

"I wanted to make sure that she's up for it. I don't want her to have a relapse when I'm there. I'm to understand that she's doing much better." He told his dad to go slow and that she was doing better than he could have imagined. "Good deal then. I'm so happy that you were there when you guys were set to help her. Thank goodness for Mac, too."

"Yes, there is no telling how long she might have been there without the proper care before she died. I hate to think about that, but that's exactly what would have happened. And with her moving away, there is no telling how long before anyone would have found her. That scares me, too."

After hanging up with his dad, Kahana made his way home again. He was exhausted; however, this time, he was physically drained rather than just mentally. As soon as his head hit the pillow this time, he was out.

Chapter 8

Axel loved the way things were moving along. His business was nearly finished, just waiting on furniture and some décor to make it look better than he thought it would look if he'd just left everything bare. Thank goodness for his mom, or he might well have never thought of the finishing touches that she put everywhere. Mac helped so she could find the things that mom was looking for, but she didn't do foo-foo, as she called it.

After getting things in the filing cabinet, not that much right away, he looked around and felt very proud of what was going on in there. He might well never take on a partner, but he thought that the rooms, for one, were just as good-looking as the rest of the place was looking. That's when his thoughts went to Debra.

She had been done wrong. Not only did she not get the money that had been promised her but the law firm that she was to get wasn't even there anymore. The building, along with nearly everything in it, had been seized by the courts until such time as a hearing could be set up for Phil—he decided to call him that as well when he figured out that it pissed him off. He'd claimed the building that had been Debra's uncle and had cleaned it out of every scrap of paper, file, and furniture. Claiming that it was all his before the will could be read seemed like a logical thing because Debra couldn't be gotten in touch with at the time.

Axel had filed for Debra when she'd been in the hospital and had gotten a judgment against Phil and all parties involved in order for him to not take over the firm. Not that he could. Without at least a law degree, he couldn't own the firm anyway. There were a lot of things going on that he didn't care for.

First of all, it seemed that the firm that had been handling the will didn't work very hard to find out where Debra was. However, they did notify her that the uncle had died. Also, and this one boggled his mind more, the firm handling the estate, which was quite large, allowed Phil to go in and take over the firm's assets like he'd inherited it.

Then, there was the money as well as the home that she was to inherit. The firm, instead of holding the house in her name, had allowed Phil to not just move in but he'd been able to put his name on the deed as sole owner. Either he had something over the other firm, or they were about as incompetent as he thought. There was no way that he'd allowed any of the things going on to happen had he been in charge.

The past was the past, as his dad was so fond of saying, and put your foot forward and make it right from where you came in. And he planned on doing that. As soon as Debra signed off on him being her attorney. He was hoping to get that done today, as a matter of fact.

He didn't know why he felt so protective of her. She was a nice woman and seemed to have her shit together. Intelligent too. He liked that they could have a conversation, and neither of them felt like they had to explain everything. It sounded arrogant, he knew, but it was nice. It was much like his own wife. They just seemed to click into place. He answered his phone when it rang.

"It's Debra Author. I have a question for

you. Well, several, but this one will make way for the others. How much will it cost me to have you represent me when I go to court in a couple of days? Remember, you know as much about my finances—more than likely more than I do." He told her that he was doing this because he liked her. "I'm not sure if you understand this or not, but you won't make any money by doing things like this for free. I mean, sure, you have all the money in the world compared to me, but I have to pay you something."

"How about we work on that when you come over tonight for dinner." She asked him if she'd missed something as she was still in the hospital. "I forgot about that. By the way, you sound so much better than the last time I spoke to you. I'll talk to you about it when you're home. Right now, I'm filing judgments against the firm that represented your uncle and his estate, the state as well as your cousin. He won't be able to do anything else until the hearing is over. Which a part of me hopes is a long time. He's also been arrested. I think you know that. He's been moved out of the house by the police as well, and all the locks have been changed. I have the keys here, as well as the judge who is presiding over this. I don't want you to stress out or anything, but to me, this looks like it's going to go all your way." She asked him about the will. "They read the one that Phil had in his possession instead of getting the one that was filed. That's going to cost them a great deal of money, if not put them out of business. I've seen parts of the will. The entire estate was to go to you with the stipulation that you marry within one year before or after his death. I don't know your personal situation, but I'm having that looked into as well. He can say that you marry, but I don't know anything about that, as I said."

For whatever reason, Kahana popped into his head. Shaking his head, not sure why that came to mind, but he wasn't going to go down that road right now. He could hear the stress building up in her voice and was glad that she started doing the breathing like she'd been taught. He could her stress begin to get to her and she did the breathing like she'd been taught to calm herself.

In through her nose and out through her mouth. She did that several times while she was supposed to be thinking of the most serene place that she could think of. He wondered where it would be. His would be home on the couch with Mac. Then again, Kahana popped into his head.

"Are you better?" After telling him what she was doing, except for the part where his brother was there in his own thoughts, he spoke to her again. "You take your time, Debra. Anything that I have to say to you can wait until you're better. Just breathe."

"You're all so nice to me." She started to cry then, and he knew that she was embarrassed. He would have been had it been himself in the hospital without anywhere to go when she came out. "I don't know what I'd do without your family around. I know that you've saved my life, but you've become so much more important to me than that. Am I making sense?"

"Yes. Believe it or not, I feel the same way about you. Even Mac said she thought of you as her long-lost sister, one that she could love." They both laughed, and he felt so much better because of it. "There you go. Laughter is the best medicine, or so I've been told. How about you rest a little while and I'll come in and talk to you tomorrow. I do need you to sign off on a couple of things, and that shouldn't be too much. I'll even spring for some lunch. Are you on a special diet?"

"Yes, cardiac diet. No salt, no caffeine. Pretty much anything that tastes good is out." Again, the two of them laughed. "I can have treats if I want them. It's worse, they said that I deny myself anything. Then I'll binge on them. But I'm to be careful from now on what I put into my gut."

"I don t know that I'd survive on a diet like that. I'm too much of a snacker, too. I'm assuming those are out, like chips and dip?" She told him that they were, and that wasn't going to bother her overly much as she wasn't much of a snacker anyway. "Good for you. I'll see what I can bring in for you. I looked up the kind of diet you're on, and I think I can make that work for something to be brought to you. Do you need anything else?"

She asked him where Kahana was, and he had to hold back his laughter this time. She did like him, he thought, and that might be the best thing for her. When he told her that he was making rounds at the hospital for a doctor who had gotten ill, she told him that she was being foolish thinking that he'd come by to see her like she was his only patient.

"You like him, don't you?" She wanted to

deny it, but in the end, she didn't for which he was happy about. All she told Axel was that she felt better when he was around. Calmer. "My wife does that for me as well. Makes my temper better, and she holds my hand and I feel like I can conquer the world. She'd smack me for saying this, but sometimes, I want to start an argument with her just to see her temper flare up. She has a good one, too."

After talking to her about a few more things, he did tell her that the things that were at her apartment were now in his garage. Also, the things that had stickers on them—he thanked her several times for those added notes. They had been distributed to all the places that she'd marked them as going. She then thanked him several more times before she told him that the nurse was in the room and she needed her vitals. After hanging up, he sat at his desk, trying to think of a way that would bring Kahana and Debra together. It bothered him some that her home seemed to be in Tennessee but he thought that with a little persuading, they could convince her to stay around here and make a life with his brother—if it came to that, he thought.

He and Mac were having their families

over for dinner tonight. It was too hot out to have anything out of doors but they were able to make it work by opening up the patio doors that had just been installed this morning so that it looked like they were outside. Axel loved their new home and was more than happy that they'd been able to get it all finished up in a reasonable time.

"I wanted to ask you something about your brothers." He looked up from his desk to see Mac there and realized that his computer had gone to sleep at some point. "Are any of your brothers seeing anyone they might consider special? I mean, you know, more than one date in the last decade?"

"Not that I'm aware of. But I've only just gotten off the phone with Debra, and she mentioned to me that she was calmer when Kahana was around. Then she told me that she liked him, but that was all. Why? What do you have planned?" She told him that she'd not really had a plan other than to make sure that she invited them to dinners, too. "I don't know that any of them would want that. We've all been pretty close to the chest about people being invited to our homes. I don't remember one time that any of us have ever had a date over to have dinner with us. Ever. I don't know why, but that's the way things have been."

"You mean your parents have never met your girlfriends? That's kind of nice, I guess. You don't want someone to stick around if they're not missed, right, I suppose. Now that I think about it, I've never had anyone over to my old place either. It just didn't seem right for whatever reason." He asked her about benefits. "I've never done that either. I've had sex, but it's been a quickie at their home or a hotel. When I think about that, I'm lucky that I've never ended up dead. I was insane, I think."

"Not insane, but a little too trusting. I know how that is. Sometimes, when I talk to a person that I'm to represent, I find myself sometimes, not all the time, believing everything they tell me. But the saying that there are two sides to every story is true. Even that sometimes can be troublesome for me." She laughed when he did. "I've gotten jaded over the years, too. I don't have any patience anymore nor do I have much in the way of sympathy for people. My family, yes, but clients? Not so much. They'll lie right to my face and think that's just fine and dandy."

"You're not like that now. At least you

weren't with me." He said that he'd known something was going on between them before he realized that he loved her. "Very romantic that. Thank you. But I have to go and see some people at the hospital about some things that are going on with the reno that we did for them a few years ago. They want one of the rooms to be larger than it is now, but without knocking down a couple of walls, that's not going to happen. They should have thought of the sizes of the rooms before putting in the plans. My dad tapes out a room size on the ground or floor to allow people to see what it is they're getting. I might start that practice as well. Then I need to go and see my grandmother. I don t want to, I even told her that I'd not be back but the station house is begging me to come by to tell her to shut up. I think they're slightly afraid of her for some reason. Did you want to come with me?"

"I'll gladly go with you to see your grandmother, but I can't make it to the hospital right now. If I don't get this paperwork cleared away, I'm going to be behind more than I am right now." She told him that was what she'd been hoping for. "Did you hear that they're looking for a replacement for the hospital head nurse position?

Dad and Mom are going to pay for background checks on them just so they can have peace of mind over this. It's a royal fuck up if you ask me."

"I know. So much is going on you have to wonder if it will be better off closing down the place and starting over. But I also know that they do good work there, too. Just a few bad people making things difficult for a lot of people. You forever hear about the bad but seldom the good in people, I believe."

When Mac left him in order to get the hospital straightened out, Axel dug deeper into his work to get it all cleared away. He also made notes of things that he still needed in their home if he was going to be able to work from here daily. Also, he needed to hire himself someone to answer the phones at the new building if he was ever going to get any new clients. However, right now, he didn't care if he had any or not. Hanging out with Mac more than made up for working outside of the house.

~*~

It took her longer than she thought it would take at the hospital. They wanted her to make all the rooms in the place be able to handle two patients at a time. They'd only just gotten finished with it being done up for one person per room now they didn't like that. Too bad. She wasn't a magician, and she wasn't going to be able to pull more room out of her ass like it seemed that they wanted her to.

Since she needed to vent, she told Axel that she was going to see her grandmother on her own. She wanted her to pick a fight with her, and that would help with her stress. Since meeting Debra, she had been watching her food intake as well as her stress levels. The poor girl was only a couple of months younger than her, and she'd had a heart attack already.

"There you are. What's taken you so long? Or do you not have respect for your elders." She didn't bother answering her grandmother as she wouldn't hear it anyway. Instead, she asked her what she wanted. "Right to the point. I like that. I don't like you but I do respect your ability to get to the point."

"Yet here you are going on about shit when I told you that I didn't have all day when you had the station call me. What is it, Grandmother? I've got a long list of things that I need taken care of and—"

"If I keep you here all day, that's what it takes for you to listen to my demands. I want you to talk to your father about paying me more money. I need to live, too, and he has it all. Had I known that that stupid husband of mine would have done me dirty like he did, then I'd not have married him in the first place." Mac told her that without being married to him, this conversation wouldn't have to be talked about. "What are you talking about? Of course, it would have. I want what's coming to me and I don't like that I'm being denied things that well should have come to me in the first place."

"Now, on that, we can agree. I want you to get what's coming to you as well." Nodding, Grandmother told her it was about time that someone thought that she was done dirty. "I think you misunderstood me. I want you to get what's coming to you by way of the law. You're not a nice person and I cannot stand to be around you. You're mean, manipulative as well as a rotten soul. I'm not going to help you ruin my family. I love that you're in jail, and I hope that you have to stay here until you die of meanness."

What are you talking about? People don't

die from meanness. What a thing to say to me. Of
course, I have to be stern about things. If I wasn't
around, everything in this place would be in ruin.
Why you should see the way that they serve food
here. They put it right on the floor and shove it
right at you. And let me tell you about the food
that is here. I've been trying for a week to get them
to bring me a nice salad and a glass of wine. It's
not like they couldn't run into Columbus to get
me one. But they won't cater to my needs like they
should be." Mac asked her why she thought that.
"What do you mean? Why shouldn't they cater to
me? I'm a very important person, and as soon as
my son gets his head on right, I'll have the money
that I have coming to me."

"About that money you think that you have
coming to you. What about the stash that you have
in the bank? Or the money that was found in boxes
all around your retirement home?" She asked how
she'd found out about that. "I'm finding out all
kinds of things about you. We, Dad, and I, had
to go and collect your things from the assisted
living home because you've been evicted. Not
only because no one liked you there but you've
not made a single payment to the place since you

moved in. By the way, you had just enough cash in the several boxes to pay that debt off."

"You listen here. If even one dollar of that money is missing, I'm going to own you. That's all mine. And I will not have you going through my things either. That is mine, and I will not be kicked out or evicted, as you said, because they got a burr up their bottom and think they can kick me out. As I said before, they couldn't run that place without me there."

"That's what they said you'd say. And you can't not pay them for living there because you were giving unsolicited advice to them. But I took care of that. Also, your phone bill. How did you get by for four years without paying that bill?" She told her that she had her ways. "I'm sure you do. But I paid that bill along with all the others that people had for you. Christ, when I think about how much was in the apartment you lived in, I want to smack the shit out of you."

Mac went over all the things that she'd been able to pay off with the money that had been stashed around in not just the apartment that she lived in but also the storage unit that she didn't pay on monthly too. While Grandmother didn't say, she knew how she'd gotten away with so much. She was a monster of the worst kind. One of the cable gentlemen who had come to turn off her cable and phone had had his family threatened to be killed. Especially his children.

"The money that is in the bank now will be used to pay for your legal fees. Not that I think you'll have enough, but we can always sell off your crap to get a bit more. Why did you think that—you know what? Never mind. I don't want to hear you going on about how you think for some reason that you're simply owed those things because you're a monster."

"I'm no such thing, and I demand that you stop calling me that." Mac rolled her eyes at her grandmother, thinking that this was much more fun than she thought it should have been. Getting to blow her off was a blast, she thought. "I have a few things that you're going to do for me. First and foremost, you're going to get all my money back and then put it all back in that apartment. I know that it's beneath me to live there, but for now, it had suited me. If you know what's good for you, you'll simply keep your mouth shut and do as you're told. I'd hate to have something happen to you and that supposed husband that you have. He's an attorney, you told me. Good, I'll have to use him. He's going to do just what I tell him to do, too."

She only half listened to what she was saying. It was boring, to say the least, and she simply didn't care what the old bat wanted. As she'd told her before, she was glad that she was in jail and not bothering anything. Tuning into her when she heard her say her name, she looked at her.

"Christ, when did you get so old?" She'd not meant to say it aloud, but now that it was out there, she didn't want to pull it back in. While grandmother was gaping at her like a fish out of water—only just now understanding what that meant, she continued on with her observation. "They must not allow you to have your hairdresser around to touch up your roots. Your hair is looking positively ancient not to mention unkept. The green jumper does nothing for your skin tone, either. Just how much makeup do you wear all the time that makes you look halfway decent."

"You take that back right now." She told her that she wasn't and didn't care if she threatened her or not. "You will when I'm out of here. You'll see what I'm talking about. Why my son had another child in you, I'll never know. At least Charles knows better than to come around with his hand out."

"I've never done that either. Nor has Dad." She sputtered around about it was a figure of speech. "That makes what you said make even less sense. You're off your rocker if you think that anything that you're saying to me is going to mean a damned thing. I've not respected nor loved you—that's right, I don't love you. I don't even like you, and I haven't since I was six years old, and you slapped me in the face because I didn't want to eat my peas. I still don't, as a matter of fact. I hate them. Mostly due to you."

"I'd have slapped you around more if not for your stupid father catching me doing it. After that, I knew I was going to have to be more careful about how I disciplined you." Mac grinned, knowing that she'd not done anything to her because she avoided her like the plague. "That stupid brother of yours went off and got married too. Then he had to breed. That woman that he's married to is nothing but a milksop. She should have been destroyed before she even made it to the womb. The same as you."

"Well then, I'm lucky that you weren't around." Her cell phone rang, and she could see Axel's face there. She also noticed the time. She needed to get out of here before dinnertime and get some nice hugs from her husband.

Axel would know just what to do when she needed comfort, too. Standing up, ignoring her demands that she sit back down, Mac answered her phone with a smile on her face. Taking her chair with her, she walked down the hallway and to the front of the station house so that she could go home. Before leaving, however, she told them not to send any more phone calls to their home. No one was coming back here to put up with her shit.

On her way home, she stopped at the state store to pick up something for them to have with dinner. There was a wine cellar in their home, but it was empty as far as she knew, and also, she didn't think that anyone had been down there for years. Picking up a box of expensive chocolates, too, she was on her way home. Calling Axel back, she told him what she'd done.

"Wonderful. You must have read my mind. I was just thinking about a nice glass of wine myself. Where are you?" She told him she was just passing the grocery store. "I ordered some dinner for us, too. Some steaks to have on the grill. I want to celebrate tonight. I got my desk cleared off, and all the motions that I needed to have filed have been filed."

She told him that she'd stop and pick it all up. "By the way, Grandmother knows about the money that was found and what was paid off. I know that they record everything at the jail, so there won't be any denying it when this goes to court. Have you had any luck getting statements from the people at the assisted living place?"

"More than I thought I'd get. About five dozen of the people living there not only sent things to me registered mail, but they had them certified, too, along with any bills that she might well owe to them." She said good. "Also, I'm sure you told her that her things are in storage. We're going to have to sell that stuff off, too, in order to pay for some other things that have come up. Honey, let's not talk about her anymore. I want us to have a nice, stressless evening and then go to bed to make love the rest of the night."

"Sounds like a great plan." Going into the grocery store, she was able to pick up the four bags of things that he'd ordered. Mac loved living in a small town like this one. Everyone knew what was going on in your life, but they seemed just as determined to help you get out of things, too. She loved the little grocery store, too.

After getting home and picking up some items that Axel hadn't ordered, she was thrilled that he came to meet her in the driveway to carry all the things that she'd purchased today. He noticed the little tests that she'd gotten, too.

"I'm late, and you and I need to know before the town does. I'd be surprised if it's not all over town that I picked up some pregnancy tests. We'll do them after dinner." He told her now, she was going to do it now. "All right. I love you, Axel Hathaway. So very much."

"And I love you, Mac Hathaway, too. More than I think that there are words in the world to tell you how I feel." He grinned. "Go do your thing with those tests. I want to know if I'm going to be a dad or not."

She hoped they were both going to be

parents. It would be something else that would piss off her grandmother if she ever found out. She might have to have one of the officers at the jail let it slip that she was. It might be worth it, she thought, just to go in and tell her that.

Before You Go...

HELP AN AUTHOR

write a review

THANK YOU!

Share your voice and help guide other readers to these wonderful books. Even if it's only a line or two, your reviews help readers discover the author's books so they can continue creating stories that you'll love. Log in to your favorite retailer and leave a review. Thank you.

AWARD WINNING, BESTSELLING AUTHOR

Kathi Barton, a winner of the Pinnacle Book Achievement Award and a best-selling author on Amazon and All Romance books, lives in Nashport, Ohio, with her husband, Paul. When not creating new worlds and romance, Kathi and her husband enjoy camping and going to auctions. She can also be seen at county fairs with her husband, an artist and potter.

Her muse, a cross between Jimmy Stewart and Hugh Jackman, brings her stories to life for her readers in a way that has them coming back time and again for more. Her favorite genre is paranormal romance, with a great deal of spice. You can visit Kathi online and drop her an email if you'd like. She loves hearing from her fans. aaronskiss@gmail.com.

Follow Kathi on her blog: http://kathisbartonauthor.blogspot.com/

www.ingramcontent.com/pod-product-compliance
Lightning Source LLC
Chambersburg PA
CBHW032005170626
46807CB00006B/2662